LOCKDOWN HORROR #1

Compiled & Edited by

D. Kershaw | Maggie Pawsey | S.N. Graves

Also available and coming soon from Black Hare Press

DARK DRABBLES ANTHOLOGIES

WORLDS   APOCALYPSE
ANGELS   LOVE
MONSTERS   HATE
BEYOND   OCEANS
UNRAVEL   ANCIENTS

BHP WRITERS' GROUP SPECIAL EDITIONS

STORMING AREA 51
EERIE CHRISTMAS
BAD ROMANCE
TWENTY TWENTY

OTHER VOLUMES
DEEP SPACE
WHAT IF?
KEY TO THE KINGDOM
DEEP SEA
BEYOND THE REALM

Twitter: @BlackHarePress
Facebook: BlackHarePress
Website: www.BlackHarePress.com

LOCKDOWN HORROR #1 title is
Copyright © 2020 Black Hare Press
First published in Australia in April 2020 by Black Hare Press

The authors of the individual stories retain the copyright of the works featured in this anthology

All characters and events in this publication, other than those clearly in the public domain, are fictitious and any resemblance to real persons, living or dead, is purely coincidental.

All rights reserved. No part of this production may be reproduced, stored in a retrieval system, or transmitted, in any form or by any means, electronic, mechanical, photocopying, recording or otherwise, without the prior permission of the publisher and copyright owner.

Paperback : ISBN 978-1-925809-98-5

Cover design	Dawn Burdett	www.dmburdett.com
Formatting	Ben Thomas	www.blackharepress.com
Editing	D. Kershaw	www.blackharepress.com
	Maggie Pawsey	
	S.N. Graves	www.sngraves.com
Read Team	David Green	davidgreenwritercom.wordpress.com
	Jennifer Hatfield	jhatfieldauthor.wixsite.com/website
	Jodi Jensen	jodijensenwrites.wordpress.com
	Lyndsay Ellis-Holloway	authorlyndseyellisholloway.webador.co.uk
	Stacey Jaine McIntosh	www.staceyjainemcintosh.com

TABLE OF CONTENTS

ONLY EVER NIGHT

By L.P. Hernandez

Derek dreamed of the carnival throughout the night, the blinking lights and swirling colours. He smacked his lips at the remembrance of deep fried dough, dusted with sugar. It was a night of fun, a night to forget the crops now wilted in the fields, the milk cow, whose calf was stillborn with eyes like pond water. He burned through his pennies quicker than he planned, but even with his money spent it was better to be there than the farm.

He roused with calliope music still tinkling in his ears. Though he heard his father's heavy footsteps elsewhere in the house, it must have been a mistake, a final tendril of the dream slipping silently into the dark. His eyes fell to the window, which was cracked and the curtains partially drawn. There was no murky morning light leaking through, and so Derek turned over and fell back into dreams.

The dreams had only minutes to take root before other sounds disturbed his sleep. Derek yawned and stretched, his head cocked curiously at the window. It was still night. The visible portion of the window was but a black rectangle.

His sister's abrupt snore drew his attention in her direction. Her back was to him, and her hair, the same copper-red as the deer that meandered through their dying fields, appeared black in the dark. There was only one clock in the house, and it rested on the mantle above the fireplace, but Derek knew it was later in the morning than it seemed.

"Wilma!" Derek whispered.

The girl flinched but did not rouse.

"Wilma, wake up!" Derek said.

Her snore tapered off and she flipped onto her back. Derek swivelled his legs off the bed and padded to her, the dusty wooden floors squeaking beneath him. There were sounds of commotion from the kitchen, his mother and father speaking softly to each other.

Derek touched Wilma's shoulder.

"Wilma, are you awake?"

She blinked and stared at the ceiling.

"Hey, something's going on."

She licked her lips and mumbled, "What?"

Derek looked to the window again.

"It's dark outside."

Wilma followed his gaze to the window, "So?"

"Something's going on. Let's go," he said, and walked to the door.

She followed behind as he stepped into the hall. Their parent's voices were low, purposefully so. The pair tip-toed into the living room and saw their parents standing in the doorway, staring out at the lawn. The words were louder, but no clearer.

Derek glanced at the clock and nudged Wilma.

"What?" she whispered.

He pointed to the clock. At seven years old she was old enough both to tell time and to understand it was still dark when it shouldn't be.

"We're late for school," she said.

"I don't know if that matters right now."

They walked through the living room and stood behind their parents, listening for a moment before announcing themselves.

"…make a lick of sense. I suppose I should go to town," their father said.

Their mother stiffened at the suggestion.

"Are you sure? What if something bad is happening?"

"Only one way to find out," he said, turning and noticing the children.

"What is it, Dad?" Derek asked.

Daryl shook his head, "Don't rightly know, son. Clock's not wrong, that's for sure. Been waiting for sunrise for a couple hours now."

"Are we safe?" Wilma asked.

Her mother kneeled so she was eye-level with the girl. She spread her arms, and Wilma walked into the embrace.

"We will be, baby."

Derek joined his father on the porch. Inside, Wilma's attention was diverted to breakfast. Only a few hens laid eggs anymore, and about half of those were bad. Darlene pulled the curtains above the kitchen and hoped Wilma might forget about the darkness.

"What do you make of it?" Derek asked.

Every day he seemed to grow a little taller, despite the lack of protein in his diet. They both stared at the field, the silhouettes of cornstalks turning to dust.

"I don't know, son. I do think we ought to go to town and see what others are saying. Maybe there's a reason for it."

"Should we turn on the radio?"

The moon was nearly full, its topography obscured by its brightness. Daryl squinted at it. There was something different, something off he sensed but could not describe. Before he had a chance, he heard the scream from inside.

They bolted into the kitchen.

"Daryl?"

Darlene held an egg in her hand, only the shape was wrong. He moved closer to inspect. Darlene's hand trembled, the egg rocked back and forth across her palm. It was half an egg, a little less, but the shell was still intact.

It was disappearing.

"Daryl?" she cried.

He plucked the egg from her hand and held its dwindling form between his thumb and forefinger. Over the course of half a minute, his fingers came closer and closer together as the egg evaporated into the air. There was no sound. There were no errant particles floating about.

His thumb and forefinger touched. The egg was gone.

***

They packed into the old Ford, not bothering to change into proper clothes. In the ten minute journey to town, no one spoke. Each wrestled with the idea of a disappearing egg, wondering how it was connected to the absence of daylight. There were only a handful of streetlamps in their small town, and those did little to repel the darkness.

There was a crowd outside of the police station; farm families wearing robes and pyjamas. Daryl parked the Ford and the family rushed toward the throng.

"I'm telling you, Jack, it ain't a police matter," the sheriff said.

He held his hands up as the crowd responded with murmured jeers.

"Then what sort of matter is it?" Jack said, fear causing his voice to shake.

"I can't control the weather."

"Can't you call someone? Can't you ask Denver about it?"

The crowd murmured in support of this idea.

The sheriff lowered his hands but

glanced at his watch as he did. He looked down the street, over the heads of the crowd.

"You're not going to do *anything*?" a new voice added.

The sheriff removed his hat to run his fingers through his hair. His hesitation was obvious, and the crowd picked up on it.

"What are you not telling us?" Jack asked.

Daryl weaved his way to the front of the crowd. He and the sheriff had been friends since high school.

"Bill, what is it? What do you know?" Daryl asked.

The sheriff sighed and nodded for a moment.

"Can't call anyone. Phones don't

work. Radios are only picking up static."

He swallowed hard.

"What else, Bill?" Daryl asked.

The sheriff stared at his boots.

"I sent Hank and Roger out. Sent 'em over to Cheyenne Wells."

"Yeah? What did they find?"

Bill shook his head, "I don't think they made it. Had a little back and forth over the radio, then they stopped answering. Been two hours now. Only static."

Without discussing it, the crowd navigated a block down the street to the church. It was Friday, at least it should have been, but they filed in and took their normal places in the pews as if it were Sunday morning. Pastor John stood at the lectern scribbling notes in his bible.

The room was lit with lantern light, which carved flickering shapes into the darkness. On a typical Sunday morning there was enough light from outside the lanterns were not necessary at all.

Pastor John dabbed at his nose with a handkerchief and began to read. He read several passages about the Lord being a light in the darkness, to little effect. A few more townsfolk filed in and lingered in the back of the room. Pastor John acknowledged them with a head nod and returned to the verses.

"That's all good, John, but what are we supposed to do? Does it say anything about that?" a man asked.

"Now hold on, Sam, I'm trying to be a comfort here," Pastor John said, then flipped to a new passage.

"So, you don't know?" Sam said.

He was seated in the front pew, burly arms crossed over his barrel chest.

"What's happening? No, the Bible doesn't talk about what's happening in Colorado in 1936. I'm doing my best," Pastor John answered.

Before Sam could speak the rear doors flew open. The church filled with screams of panic, and a blurry figure raced to the front. Women hugged their children to their sides and more than one man reached for a gun he had not brought.

Her name was Beth. She was an unwed teen mother, a status that might have been a stain in another small town. It was not for her, though. The town rallied around her and pitched in with little Daisy when they could. Sometimes, anonymous milk deliveries were left on her doorstep, other times fresh-baked bread still warm from the oven. In those lean times this was no small sacrifice.

She stammered, her words jumbled in her mouth.

She held the bundle—the pink swaddling blanket—to her breast.

"Daisy," she said as the blanket unravelled.

There was nothing there. Beth dropped the blanket and collapsed on the steps leading to the lectern.

Daryl and others rushed to her aid. When she roused a few minutes later she recounted the story. Like the others, she waited for a sunrise that did not come. She made her way into town, carrying Daisy in her swaddling blanket. Over the course of the five minute walk to town, the weight felt lighter rather than heavier. She peered into the swaddle and…

"She was gone. Just gone."

Pastor John leaned his weight onto the lectern, his eyes dancing over the text in front of him. He searched the words for something relevant, something to steady the hearts of his restless flock.

Some left their pews and meandered to the door. Others waited. Pastor John closed the book and removed his glasses.

"I could make up something about the end times. This fits, doesn't it? But the honest truth is, I don't have anything of value to say at this moment. I suggest you go to where you feel safe, if there is such a place. If praying helps your heart then do that, too."

He left the Bible on the pulpit and exited through the rear of the church. As he did, the walls echoed with fresh screams.

Sam was out of his seat and dancing in the aisle. For a moment Derek thought he was possessed by the Spirit. He hadn't seen it in their church, but knew it sometimes happened when the big revival tents passed through. In the low light it was difficult to make out precisely what the man was doing. He was spinning in his overalls and looking at something that made his eyes swell in their sockets.

Well, not exactly something. He was

looking at nothing.

"Dad?" Derek whispered.

Daryl's gaze was fixed on the man, whose arms were vanishing.

"I can still feel 'em!" Sam screamed.

Inch by inch they disappeared, as if consumed by a fire no one could see.

"Oh, my God! I can still feel 'em!" Sam screamed.

His arms were stumps and then nothing at all. He screamed, and it was an awful sound, like the cow with the dead calf. After three days of it, Daryl wanted to put her down. Sam's torso disintegrated next. He stood on tip-toe as if trying to keep his head above water.

"Tell Maddie I lov—"

His final words were cut short. In the

place where the man had stood, there were only haphazard impressions of his boots on the carpet.

***

"I think I know what it is, Dad," Derek said.

"What's that?"

Daryl passed the beer to his son. It was warm and Derek didn't care much for the taste, but it seemed important to his father they share the moment. The girls were inside using the last of their sugar to bake cookies.

"The moon. It's further away," Derek said.

It was true. It was so gradual Daryl had

not noticed. The moon was smaller than it had been a few hours before. There were less stars as well.

"It's like we're fading away," Daryl said.

"Where do you think they go?" Derek asked.

Daryl shook his head, reclaimed the beer, and finished it with one gulp.

"I don't know, son. I hope the Lord doesn't make me find out."

The cornfield was a grey haze in the light of the dwindling moon. Derek could no longer see the outline of the scarecrow he'd made the previous summer. Maybe that was gone, too.

"Dad, what's that?" Derek said, pointing.

Daryl set the beer on the step and followed the direction of his son's finger. There was a faint, white glow in the cornfield. It moved through the stalks, its shape shrinking and growing. Daryl shuddered, his back going rigid.

"I don't know, son. Let's check on the girls."

After Daryl closed the door behind them, he stayed there for a minute, peering through the peephole. He then locked the door and walked quickly to his bedroom, returning with the shotgun he kept propped against the wall.

The cookies were slightly undercooked, but that did nothing to diminish their flavour. The family sat in the living room around a crackling fireplace, eating cookies and dancing around the words they wished to say but couldn't. In five-minute intervals, Daryl left his chair to pull back the curtains and gaze into the darkness, the shotgun never leaving his hand.

The clock's hour hand indicated eight, but none knew for sure if this was morning or dusk. How long had they been awake? How much time passed?

"Daddy, what happens if we disappear?" Wilma asked.

She was curled into a ball on the couch and seemed, to Daryl, especially small and fragile in that moment. Wilma was born the year before the crops began to fail and the great walls of dust erupted from their fields and drifted east, bringing misery to Kansas and Oklahoma. He'd done his best to shield her from suffering, but he couldn't make food grow from dust, and he certainly could not purchase it with dust.

Daryl released his grip on the shotgun for a moment, propping it against his chair. His boots thundered over the floorboards despite his effort to walk softly. He crouched in front of his daughter and brushed the hair from her cheek.

"We don't need the stars, my love. I'd rather count your freckles," he said, tapping the bridge of her nose.

She smiled and squirmed away from him. Had the circumstances been different it would have been a joyous time, the family with full bellies, no worries about the wilted plants or bad eggs.

"Mom?" Derek said, voice quivering.

She was still smiling, a genuine smile that reached all the way to her eyes.

"Yes?"

Derek left his place by the fire and reached a hand out. Darlene tried to take it, her serene gaze quickly turning to horror. As with the egg, as with Sam in the church, she was disappearing.

"Mommy!" Wilma scrambled over the cushions.

Derek and Daryl wrapped their arms around her.

Her chest rose and fell, and Derek heard the furious beating of her heart as he laid his head atop it.

"It's okay. It's okay. It doesn't hurt. It doesn't hurt. Wherever I'm going, look for me when you get there. It's okay. It's okay," she said.

"I love you, Mommy, don't go!" Wilma squealed.

Derek sobbed quietly as there was less and less of her to hold.

The family, reduced by one member, met in an embrace. Wilma's entire small body shook, tears and snot flowing freely, as the reality that their family was not immune settled in. In hours, minutes, or seconds she might begin to disappear.

WHUMP

Dust fell from the ceiling and a book toppled off the mantle. Daryl looked to the window. His eyes darted to the shotgun, but he did not leave his children.

"I'm s-scared, Daddy. I don't want to

disappear."

Daryl balled his hands into fists. He could not beat this phenomenon into submission. He could not shoot it with his shotgun. He could only hold the girl and hope it would not be for the last time.

The emotional toll settled into their bones as exhaustion. Derek and Wilma shared a bed for the first time in years as Daryl patrolled the house, shotgun in hand. He found streaks on the living room window; a slimy trail left by something he could not see.

****

There was a clattering sound, which pulled Derek from sleep, and his gaze immediately fell to the window. His body stiffened. It was white as bone, with a head like a horse stripped of its skin. As its nostrils flared, it blew mucus onto the window. Its tongue, the same pearly white, probed the window glass, twisting and turning. And then it was gone.

There were sounds from outside, almost insect-like. Skittering noises mixed with chirps. Derek eased from beneath his sister's arm. He watched the window as he padded out of the room. There was little light in the main body of the house, just a hint of orange from the few coals left in the fireplace.

"Dad?" Derek whispered.

He searched his parent's bedroom by feel, still whispering for his father. He was not there. He was not in any of the rooms. There was a scrap of paper in the fireplace, its edges charred but some of the writing still legible.

We wait for dawn, we pray for light,

For we are alone, and it is only ever night.

Derek found the shotgun on the floor in front of the locked front door of the house, where his father stood guard until…

The weapon still held a bit of his father's warmth. He claimed it, and his father's post, placing his eye to the peephole.

Beyond the porch there was nothing but pitch black. No grey cornstalks. Nothing.

Derek unlocked the front door. He

aimed the shotgun and passed through it, stepping out onto the porch. There was no difference in the world he saw with his eyes closed. He walked down the steps, and the sound of wood creaking caused a ripple effect in the insect noises both near and far. The fine hairs along the nape of Derek's neck stood erect.

The moon was all that remained in the night sky. It was a single point of light, a tiny, glowing grain of sand. All the stars were gone.

But he was not alone.

The clicks and chirps echoed over and around him. He recalled a Biology lesson about bats and how they navigated through the dark. He did not remember the term for it but wondered if there were horse-headed creatures nearby who could see him just fine.

Inside, Derek added the last of the logs to the embers. He nudged Wilma awake and told her about her father. She wept, quietly, into his shoulder as he watched the window. When she was done, they returned to the living room, moths to the flame.

WHUMP

The house shook from the impact. Insect noises followed, then a second WHUMP from their parent's bedroom.

"I'm scared, Derek," Wilma said.

"Me too."

As they sat, huddled together, shotgun nearby, Wilma began to hum.

"What is that?" Derek asked. "The song."

"Hm? Oh, I don't remember."

Derek remembered. It was the carnival music.

From his parent's bedroom a WHUMP was followed by the sound of glass splintering.

"Come on. I have an idea," Derek said.

They changed out of their pyjamas in the darkness of their shared bedroom. Derek escorted his sister to the old Ford. There were whispers and wet clicks all around them.

"I'll be back. Two seconds."

He darted back inside the house, which was the only source of light now that the moon was gone, and emerged brandishing a flaming log. It swivelled back and forth at the end of the poker. He roared as he flung it into the cornfield, which was as dry as autumn leaves. Thin white bodies with oversized heads fled the conflagration.

"Why did you…" Wilma began, but she was transfixed.

Derek thought for a moment, watching as the fire spread across the brittle grass of the front yard and licked the porch steps.

"For Dad. When I was little, before you were born, he loved the fields. Loved the work. But, that was a long time ago. Now he's gone, and so are the fields."

They drove down the dirt path to town, the headlights stabbing cones through the darkness. Wilma rambled about childish things, her mood shifting from happy to mournful. Near the edge of town, Derek eased the car to a stop.

It stood in the road within a cloud of dust kicked up by the Ford. It was taller than a man though its back was hunched, as if accustomed to stooping in caverns with low ceilings. Its skin, now coated with Colorado dirt, was grey like the slugs Derek sometimes used as bait for fishing.

It turned its head to the side, showing a wide canal where ears might have been on a horse. Wilma dug her fingernails into Derek's forearm, but he did not notice at the time. The creature swivelled its head back and forth, sending clicks and chirps at the car and into the darkness beyond. As Derek reached for the shotgun, the beast lumbered off the road, its knuckles grazing the ground.

Wilma was silent after that. She stared

at the black outside the window, still gripping her brother's arm. At any moment he or she might disappear. If it was inevitable, he hoped to last just a little while longer.

He reached the carnival entrance and drove through it. Some attractions were already taken down, bundled up and loaded into truck beds. There was still a faint smell of popcorn and fried dough in the air. At last, the headlights fell upon the ride Derek hoped was still standing.

They stepped out of the car into the night. Derek left the Ford's lights on, using the light to help him figure out the levers. There was a key in the generator, which sputtered to life when he turned it. The Ferris Wheel lit up, bulbs lining its borders.

Wilma shielded her eyes, smiling and turning away.

"Come on," Derek said, taking her hand and leading her up the steps.

He escorted her to a gondola and closed the door.

"What about you?" she asked, eyes wide and fearful.

Derek nodded to the panel with its various levers.

"Gotta get the thing going."

"Okay."

After a bit of trial-and-error, Derek sent the gondola to the top of the Ferris Wheel and halted it there. Then, he climbed the spokes and dropped into the gondola next to his sister.

"It's strange, isn't it?" he asked. "To

see the sky like that."

She handed him a cookie.

"I wonder where we are now," she murmured.

The calliope music combined with the chug of the generator blocked the sound of insect noises. When Derek closed his eyes, it was easy to imagine he was back at the carnival and the world was right. He could almost hear the excited chatter of children, the carnival barkers doing their best to shake the loose change from pockets of rubes.

He held his little sister around her shoulders. The Ferris Wheel was her favourite. She couldn't handle the other rides yet, not even bumper cars.

Off in the distance there was an orange

glow, the growing blaze he'd set only minutes before. If he squinted, it almost looked like a sunrise.

UNBREAKABLE

By Zoey Xolton

Emilia raises her tear-streaked face from her knees as the dim light bulb flickers, casting the cramped room under the staircase in a sickly orange glow. A single moth flutters about the swaying globe, its fragile wings battering at the glass, throwing dancing shadows against the walls. With a parched and scream-torn throat, she whispers, "You have wings, why don't you fly away from here? I would, given half a chance."

Adjusting her position, the too-tight handcuffs binding her wrists jingle, clinking against the pair secured around her ankles. The tiny room smells of dust, blood, sweat, and sex. It'd turned her stomach the first few weeks, but after being forced to sleep in her own vomit, she'd learned to suppress her revulsion.

Twice she'd been hosed off outside during the winter, under the cover of darkness, like a dog. It was the last time she remembered seeing the sky. As the icy water assaulted her naked body, she'd hugged herself against the onslaught, her tired red eyes trained on the stars above. Her flesh had been broken in ways she hadn't imagined possible, even in her worst nightmares. Yet despite the torture, abuse, and isolation, she held fast knowing that her spirit and courage could never be taken from her.

At every opportunity she would fight, not just her sick and depraved captors, but the demons that had come to torment her mind. After six months locked away, isolated in darkness—with the exception of being dragged from her lodgings, writhing and screaming, for another paying customer—she'd begun having conversations with the voices in her head.

They told her that she deserved her treatment, that she was nothing more than a collection of raw, and swollen holes, and that she existed for no other purpose than to please those who would use her and take pleasure in her suffering.

The demons of doubt sang to her in her fitful slumber, taunting, jeering—desperate to squash any glimmer of brave hope or self-respect that might surface. At times, the voices won, but only the battle, never the war. Some days when her flesh gave out, and she lay beaten and bruised, cuffed to a soiled bed, she fell away from herself, retreating to the safety of the darkness within her own mind. In those moments, she was separate—her body merely a puppet, a toy to be played with.

Victorious, the demons would crow, dancing at the outskirts of her precious, untouchable sanctuary. But when her strength returned, she would emerge like a cornered alley cat. All claws, spit, and fire she would fight until it bothered even them. She would not submit. They wanted her to relinquish her will, but she could not—would not. Physically, she fought like a warrior, until in exasperation and anger, her captors clouted her over the head, or slapped her into sweet oblivion.

The all too familiar sound of the key in the old lock rouses her from her disturbed and fitful sleep. As she looks up into the cruel blue eyes of her balaclava-wearing abductor, the demons in her head begin to chant: *Again! Again! Today will be the day you break!* In response the fire in her soul ignites, exploding within her with renewed vigour. She savours her abductor's disturbed expression as a sneer stretches her cracked lips, making them bleed.

"You can't break me," she whispers to him, as much as to the demons in her head, her voice quavering with pain, and rage. "You can try, but my suffering only makes me stronger."

"We'll see about that, Alley Cat," he retorts, ripping her to her feet.

For the rest of the day, and for the first time in months, the voices in her head fall silent.

First published in *Isolation*, Fantasia Divinity Magazine, 2019

DEATH SPORES

By Stephen Herczeg

Earth sat alone, a glittering jewel in the dark expanse of space that hides mysteries beyond comprehension. A grey chunk of rock hurtled towards the silent planet. Earth's solitude would soon be shattered.

The night sky lit up as the meteor burnt through the atmosphere. Losing altitude, it headed straight towards a messy suburban backyard. A wrenching scream of metal greeted the meteor as it punched a fist-sized hole through a car and ploughed into the dirt below.

Neal, a large, perpetually single, slob of a man, was dragged from sleep by the explosive noise.

"What the hell?" he said, looking out the window.

He rose and pulled a night shirt onto his bare torso. The ends failed to cover the expansive butt crack that poked from his pants.

Neal stepped out and surveyed the scene, noticed a dust cloud near his car, and moved towards it. Immediately he spied the hole in the roof. He threw up his hands in distress.

"My car, my beautiful car," he said.

As the torch shone through the hole, the light glinted off the metallic surface of the meteorite nestled on the ground beneath.

Neal dropped to his knees and looked under the car. The meteorite was surrounded by small, white, round orbs. He studied the nearest one. It looked like a common puffball mushroom.

"Where'd that come from?" he said.

He reached under the car and extended a finger to prod the mushroom. As he touched the orb, it exploded, shooting a stream of green spores directly into his face.

He coughed, gagged, drew air into his lungs and sucked in the entire cloud of spores. This caused even more coughing.

Neal burst into the house gasping for air. He ran to the sink and filled a glass of water, downing it in a single gulp to wash away the mushroom spores. The coughing subsided and he wiped away the stream of tears from his eyes. Filling the glass again, he drank it down and leant back against the sink, finally in control of himself.

"GROWL."

He looked around, shocked out of his stupor.

"GROWL."

He looked down. The noise came from his stomach.

"GROWL."

He grabbed at his belly. Looked at the fridge.

"Hungry," he said.

Moving to the fridge, he ripped the door open. He surveyed the contents and loaded up his arms with all he could carry. Moving to the table he dumped everything, sat down and began to feast.

***

Dawn broke, casting a shaft of light across a recumbent Neal's face. He blinked and sat up. His eyes surveyed the decimated ruins of his late night meal.

He yawned. Stretched.

"GROWL."

His face dropped in confusion.

"GROWL."

He staggered to the fridge. Opened the door. This time it was empty. He turned to the pantry. It too was empty. His eyes glanced at a small chalkboard on the pantry door, a long list of items were scrawled on it.

"Crap," he said, "shopping day."

"GROWL," his stomach added.

He grimaced and grabbed his belly.

Surprisingly for that hour of the morning, the car park of the local supermarket was crammed full of cars. Neal parked a fair way from the entrance, exited his car, and started to waddle towards the store. He had added a pair of slippers to his ensemble, but anybody following him would still cop enough of an eyeful of plumber's crack to live with them for days.

In spite of his clothing, Neal blended into the early morning ugg-boot and tracky dak wearing denizens of the supermarket. None of the other customers outside gave him a second glance.

Once inside, it was another story.

Neal grabbed a trolley and wheeled towards the snack food aisle. His thick, pudgy hands snatched packets of chips and boxes of pretzels from the shelves and threw them into the trolley until it was piled to overflowing.

He seized a large packet of chips and burst it open. Thrusting it into the child seat he took handfuls of chips and stuffed them into his mouth as fast as he could chew and began to walk to the checkouts.

An elderly lady, moving past him, screwed up her face in disgust.

"Young man, have you no manners?" she asked.

"GROWL," said Neal's stomach.

Neal sprayed a mouthful of chip crumbs at her as he said, "Hungry, okay?"

She shook her head and moved on, grumbling to herself.

As he sidled up to the checkout, Neal failed to notice the look of distrust that bloomed across the face of the security guard manning the exit. Ignorant of the guard's interest in him, Neal simply unloaded the trolley onto the conveyor belt.

***

The pretty young checkout girl looked at the low nutritional content food coming towards her. She frowned, then looked at her new customer. A wry smile came to her face as she viewed the overweight man.

"Not following the paleo diet then?" she asked.

Neal turned to look at her.

"GROWL."

Surprised, she said, "I'll take that as a no, then," and began scanning the items.

Neal mumbled, "I'm just hungry, okay?"

He moved to the other end of the conveyor belt and loaded his trolley again, paid for his food, and headed towards the exit.

"Enjoy," she called out and smirked. The large man simply waved over his shoulder. She then caught a glimpse of his rear end. The smirk vanished.

The security guard watched Neal leave, then walked over to her.

"Did he pay for everything? Even the empty packets?" he asked.

She pressed a button and pulled a long strip of paper from her scanning machine. Nodding her head as she read, she finished with, "Yeah, everything looks to be here. Why?"

The guard turned to look at the retreating figure of Neal as he waddled away from them.

"There's just something not quite right

about him, that's all," he said.

The checkout girl grinned and said, "As compared to what?"

When the guard turned back to face her, she nodded to her right.

Standing next in line was a tall, skinny man with sleeve and facial tattoos, and numerous piercings in his lips, ears, and eyebrows.

"Fair enough," the guard said, "I still want to check him out, though." She watched him walk away before turning back to the pierced man, her friendly smile back on her face.

"Hello, handsome," she said.

***

Outside, Neal stopped and grabbed at his stomach. Another loud growl emanated from it. He tore open another packet and fed his face with chips. Several people walking past, stopped and looked. They shook their heads and continued on.

"GROWL."

Neal's face contorted with pain. He slammed more chips into his mouth. Chewed and swallowed as fast as he could to staunch the aching from his midriff.

He pushed the trolley a few more metres then stopped. He grabbed at his head. The trolley rolled on before hitting a stone and stopping.

Neal screamed. "My head. My head. Oh my God. The pain." He thrashed around where he stood. His arms flailing out then moving back to grasp at his stricken head.

People stopped near him. Their eyes transfixed on the sorrowful figure as he performed his dance of pain. An older lady moved a step closer. She slowly extended her hand towards him.

"Are you alright?" she asked in a timid voice.

"The pain. Oh my God the pain," Neal screamed.

The woman reared back and pushed herself deep into the crowd behind.

Neal dropped to his knees, his hands still clasped to his head.

The security guard ran up behind him. "Sir, are you okay? Do you need a doctor?" The growing crowd surrounding the pair inched forward. They watched; a group of voyeurs transfixed by Neal's anguish.

Neal bent down and covered his head with his arms, muffling his screams.

The guard knelt next to him and placed a hand on his shoulder. "Sir, I can get you a doctor if you'd like? It will only take a minute."

Suddenly, Neal stood bolt upright. His hands dropped from his head and hung at his sides. Trickles of blood seeped from his ears and eyes. His screams stopped. His eyes stared into space. The crowd gasped, but none uttered a word.

A single long, echoing growl broke the silence.

Neal remained perfectly still.

The crowd watched. Rapt. Waiting. Hushed.

The guard slowly stood and reached for Neal's shoulder.

Suddenly, Neal's head exploded. The guard was thrown to the ground. Blood, bone and grey matter splattered over every person crowded around. As one they reeled back in horror as the crimson rain showered them.

The guard gathered himself, stood up and stared. The rest of the crowd recovered their wits and gawked with him.

In the middle, stood the now headless body of Neal, oozing blood from the gaping neck wound. It started to sway. The knees buckled, and it collapsed to the ground with a sickening thud. Everyone stood silent, too dumbstruck to speak, even to breathe.

"GROWL."

A young girl in the crowd, her face a bloody mask of Neal's making, grabbed at her stomach.

"GROWL."

A tall man's stomach answered the call.

"GROWL."

One by one each person grasped at their stomach. Some bent over in pain. As one they all looked around at the supermarket and shuffled off on a quest to satiate their hunger.

All that was left was Neal and the security guard.

"GROWL," the security guard's stomach complained.

He looked around and eyed off the

shopping trolley full of junk food.

"Mine," he said.

First published in *Sproutlings*, Hunter Anthologies, 2016

BLACK HARE PRESS

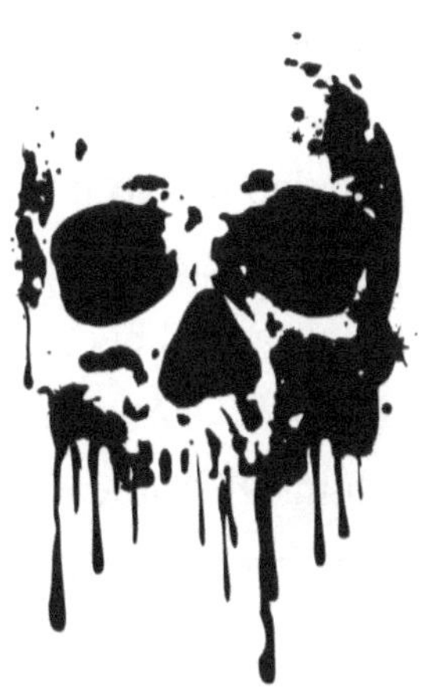

NO TOUCHING

By Amber M. Simpson

He watched her grind the pole, head thrown back, eyes closed to the music.

This one was new. Dark hair, thick thighs. Perky tits that looked natural, soft.

The front of his jeans tightened.

After her dance, they strayed to the back, where his lap replaced the pole. Her nipples dangled like candy before him. He reached and she slapped his hand.

"No touching."

He felt himself harden. He liked a challenge. Grabbing her hips, he pushed his fingers inside.

SNAP!

"I said no touching," she glared as he screamed, the stumps of his severed fingers gushing wild with blood.

First published in *Guilty Pleasures and Other Delights*, Things in the Well, 2019

HOWLS

By Galina Trefil

Patches whined with confusion, his tail tucked between his legs, as Master pounded and roared against the suburban front door.

Usually, Master gave cuddles and biscuits. He had a sweaty, homey smell that made Patches curl up, affectionate and contented, in his dirty laundry.

But now pungent decay covered Master. His veins seemed to swell against his bloated, greenish skin, so tightly that, in some places, they burst and leaked blood and foul pus across his limbs and face. That expression of his, which was so often a friendly grin, had been replaced by a frothing snarl.

When he'd tried to sink his teeth into Patches' paw, Patches had escaped through his doggy door, only to stand in his front yard, confused and hurt. Had Master just tried to…eat him? Yes! He had! And, if he could only figure out how to turn the knob on the front door, he'd be outside with Patches, trying to eat him again! Thank God, he suddenly didn't know how to do that anymore. But why? Why was Master suddenly so stupid…and mean?

Patches whimpered, looking at the other houses up and down the block, most of which had no escape routes for their pets. The yips and howls of pain and fear going on inside those abodes told him that he would be one of the few local survivors of whatever terrible event had just happened.

Were all of these Masters still human? Patches didn't know. As another ill-smelling, drooling, bipedal monster noticed him and began to give chase,

Patches fled. He would run for as long as he had to, as long as this lasted. How long would that be? Patches had always resented how most people had some degree of fear of dogs. Oh, what he would have given for those good old days now.

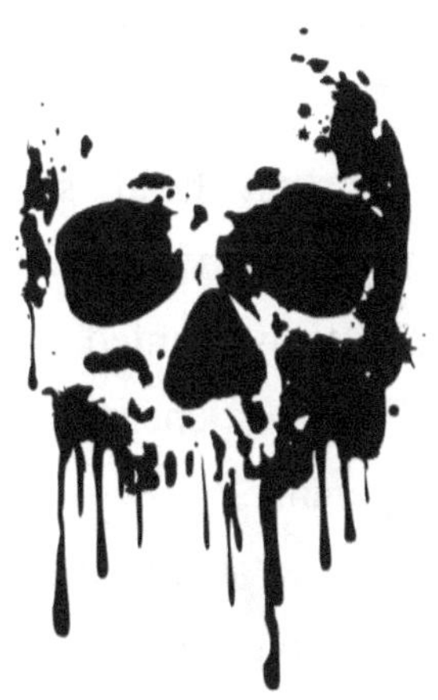

THE TEA PARTY

By Kimberly Rei

Itzalchth had warned her that possessing a human wasn't as easy as it seemed. Oh, sure, the ancient demons stepped in and out of bodies as if they were born to it, but they'd had practice. They were experts. But they were also set in their ways and no one believed in them anymore. All that head spinning and cursing in tongues was brushed off as "fake news." If one truly wanted to indulge in evil and gather souls, one had to be willing to play a long game.

Scheherazade stood over the small bed, a grin twisting her black lips. Fangs peeked out as her delight deepened. A long game indeed. The child couldn't be any more than five years old. Her delicate face was the picture of innocence. Golden curls tumbled perfectly over the pillow, golden lashes hiding what had to be blue eyes. 'Zade swallowed a cackle and shifted to smoke. As the girl took a deep, slumbering breath, 'Zade slipped into her open mouth.

She was expecting to feel the small body settle around her. That's what Itzalchth had said would happen; one would have to shift and stretch until it fit. He'd worried about her plan, warning that there may not be room in such a tiny shape.

That wasn't the problem.

A vast, desolate landscape stretched out before her. The ground was garish pink; the sky, a most horrific purple. Lime green tumbleweeds blew by riding a rotten cotton candy breeze. Scheherazade clamped a taloned hand over her mouth as her gorge rose. What Hell had she stumbled into? She began walking, looking for an out or a clue. Anything that would offer information.

She walked and walked, unable to tell the passing of time. There was nothing. No change. Just more tumbleweeds and a foul, unrelenting wind. Her head was pounding by the time huge sapphire blue eyes opened in the sky above her. A giggle crashed over her, the voice far too loud and far too high-pitched.

"Yay! I have a new friend! You can play with me for always. Just don't fall apart like the others, okay? They didn't like my games, but I know you will!"

A rushing noise chased the girl's enthusiasm. 'Zade turned to face it and watched a great wave of honey-brown water sweep towards her. As she began to run in the opposite direction, the child giggled again. "Let's have a tea party!"

THE NOCTURNAL SOLDIER

By Matthew M. Montelione

Smithtown, New York. 1784.

The American Revolution was finally

over. Young Patriot soldier Isaac Parker returned home changed by his experiences—his mind was lost in battlefields of blood; he could not sleep at night. He neglected his duties as a cooper under his father's employ and fell into a deep depression. He particularly wrestled with a juxtaposition within himself; he thought of himself as a good person, yet he felt like the only way to satisfy his unrest was to kill again, to once again taste the fruits of victory. But how? Day after day, he debated ways of placating himself, falling deeper into the dark channels of his mind, distancing himself from friends and family.

As normalcy resumed in his postwar community, Isaac realized that his fellow countrymen were not as virtuous as he once thought. He saw them violate women and children, steal, and connive against others for personal gains. These were not the ideals he fought for. Were these brutes the future of the fledgling nation he had risked his life for? He thought of a wonderful idea to remedy the situation, one that would satisfy both his virtue and bloodlust.

He began searching for evil-doers throughout Smithtown in the dead of night. During one such patrol, he caught a man trying to enter a widow's home. The man was clearly drunk, but Isaac had no pity for intoxicated fools. The soldier carefully crept behind the villain, slitting his throat in one swift motion. It was his first kill outside of battle. How glorious was the returning sweetness of victory! He smiled as the vagabond's blood flowed through his fingers and soaked the ground. After his kill, he went to the nearby lake and washed himself. He lingered long in the peaceful water, silent and at one with the night.

Thereafter, Isaac bathed in the lake after every kill. He tallied up quite the list of victims. The more he killed, the easier he slept. His careful method of cutting up the bodies, sealing them in his father's barrels, and dropping them in the water was a seamless system, the constable had no leads on any of his murders.

Unbeknownst to Isaac, one soul took notice of his efforts. Her acute attention was piqued, watching him from afar after every kill as he bathed in the lake.

One stormy night as he washed, the dark voluptuous shape of Isabella Pain rose from the water beside him.

Unalarmed, Isaac marvelled at her. Her skin was as pale as a corpse drained of blood, her long hair dripped with murky water. But she was utterly beautiful. He could not stop staring at her, his eyes gravitating first to her piercing eyes, then to her wet breasts.

Rain poured down; lightning cracked from a black cloud under a crescent moon.

"I have seen your courageous deeds from afar," Isabella cooed. "You protect women, and those who are most vulnerable. You are more of a man than any of your fellows." She drew nearer to Isaac. "Such strength," she said, brushing her cold, slender fingers down his chest.

Captivated, he wrapped his arms around her waist.

"Fight alongside me, my nocturnal soldier," Isabella said, dropping her fangs and gripping him by the head. "Together, we will wipe the Earth clean of the cowards." Fangs pierced through Isaac's soft neck.

He screamed in pleasure, and woke up the next night with renewed purpose.

DOLLY

By Erica Schaef

Cut. But the scissors lose their momentum; worn blades pinching uselessly at fine, golden tresses. The little girl shrugs and moves away from her doll, still brandishing the sheers. She is oblivious to the dull thud as her doll falls; the slight crack of fracturing porcelain.

At night, the girl sleeps soundly, her even breaths unlabored. Then a noise, soft and subtle, nonetheless causes her to start. She blinks up at the darkened ceiling. Silence.

Then, the slight rustling of fabric beside her ear; the tiniest clink of metal.

Snip. Her hair. Slice. Her face. Warm blood trickles. Dolly smiles.

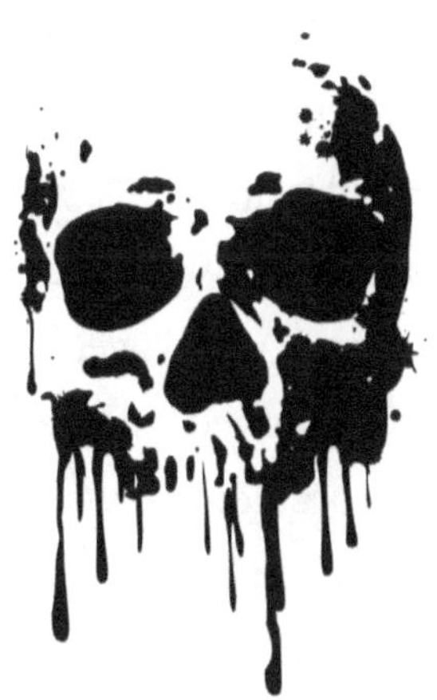

CANNIBALS OF KENTUCKY

By J.L. Royce

"You must be joking."

Boris Petronowa glared at Andy, his dark eyes shadowed by a strong brow.

The pitch was not going to plan. The

elevator's whir filled the ensuing silence, a soundtrack to the stillbirth of a young screenwriter's dream.

The producer, wrapped in a suit costing more than Andy's net worth, leaned into him and rumbled, "Here's a byline: 'They hold no prejudice—white meat from the North, dark meat from the South' Hmm?"

Andy gawped at him, dwarfed by the executive's bulk, unsure whether his comment was a serious suggestion or a cruel joke.

"It could work?" he offered.

Petronowa scowled. "You've packaged a proposal sure to offend everyone in America!" And yet, Andy reflected, the producer himself did not seem particularly shocked.

Andy pressed on. "Isn't that what reality television is about?" He felt the heat rising in his face. "And there's the scenery—the waterfalls, caves…"

He played his only remaining card.

"I've done a lot of research—found some intriguing sources, not public, documenting an *actual cult*—"

The elevator slowed. Andy broke off at a glance from Petronowa. The doors parted, and another executive stepped in.

She was smartly dressed, with a bearing that suggested she was not to be trifled with. The producer made no attempt to move, forcing the newcomer to stand close in front of him. She was as tall as Andy, with honey blonde hair wrapped atop her head. He saw the producer's hand flexing at his side, fingers inches from her hemline.

Petronowa's eyes narrowed. "Beautiful women, you say?"

The movie mogul jabbed a fat finger at the button below his own destination.

"Tell the admin in reception that I've invited you over tonight. My place; just a little gathering. Someone you should meet will be there. Who knows; you may pick up some pointers."

"Thanks!" Andy bit off any gushing gratitude—best not to show weakness.

The door slid open at thirty-two. Petronowa's lavish salt and pepper eyebrows rose, dismissing Andy with a jerk of the head towards the hall beyond.

"Tonight, then."

As the door slid shut, the producer's fingers slipped beneath the skirt in front of him, grazing electric silk as they rose.

His companion drawled, "Such *self-control*." A manicured finger pressed the *Door Close* button, and remained there.

She half-turned to glance down at him, frowning.

"You're invitin' him to the *dinner*?" In private, she let herself slip into the slow Southern drawl that had captivated Petronowa.

"Just the party," he admitted, with a shrug. "After that…we'll see."

His free hand slipped his phone out and hit a speed dial entry. With the other hand he drew her into him.

The call connected, and Petronowa brought up the phone.

"You're coming tonight, yes? Good. I need you to talk to someone. He just showed up with a spec script he's been walking around. I'm attaching it. You'll find it…fascinating."

He sent the file and closed the call, turning his attention to the woman stropping him.

The elevator's alarm rang.

"Why don't we discuss this in my office?" Petronowa suggested.

[Reel 12, June 1985]

The woman is bathing in what the locals called Fitful Falls. The water would diminish to a trickle, they said, by the end of June, not to return until spring, barring a torrential storm.

She is nude, stepping out of the cold spray to soap herself, then back in again to rinse. Her age is indeterminate; she could be eighteen or thirty-eight. In other reels, the dark rope of wet hair falls in amber-blonde waves.

Oakley had made the movie from concealment behind boulders teetering on the decaying ridge line, just above her location. He had recorded audio on a Philips cassette, which Andy had synchronized and added when he digitized the ethnologist's 8 mm movies.

Heavy breasts and a pad of belly did nothing to detract from her appeal, in

Andy's opinion.

She finishes her last rinse, ringing out her long hair—*tension*; release; *tension*; release—before winding it in a towel and flipping it over her shoulder.

Shower over, she stares directly at the camera, with a sly smile, looks through the lens and into the camera man, the ethnologist, the aroused male. The film ends abruptly; she is out of the frame, as the camera goes pointing off-angle at the trees.

Reel 12, lying on top: it was the first thing Andy happened to peruse after he'd discovered the box of film canisters and tapes. He'd listened to Oakley's simpering description of the woman—*Laurel Anne*—idolized by the middle-aged scientist. Early on Andy had been infatuated with Laurel Anne, too—*tension*; release; *tension*; release—shamelessly masturbating to the rhythm of her gliding hands.

He couldn't bring himself to do *that* any longer, not after piecing together the entire story.

"What's 'C of K'? Is that more like 'Knights of Columbus', or 'KFC'?"

He started. Julia was waggling his tablet, displaying his to-do list. Her other hand offered a bowl of salad, which she placed at his elbow

"Neither," he replied, glancing at the kale and sprouts, then refocusing on the page of script before him. Lately she had been hinting that he 'temporarily' find regular employment. There was no way

Andy could avoid this conversation.

It was, after all, her apartment.

"Well, what then? Is it that blog you hired on to write, about forgotten scientists?"

"Yes," Andy agreed immediately, seeing an exit. "As a matter of fact, yes. I had that day job—remember?—moving files for the renovation project in the department headquarters."

Decades of physical research materials had been designated for digitization and recycling: lab notebooks, videotapes, audio tapes…and films.

"Turns out the easiest place to find forgotten scientists is in the file storage room."

Julia leaned over his shoulder, fine

brown hair drifting between them. She noticed the video still running, minimized: Reel 12.

She poked the icon. The window opened with Laurel Anne spreading suds over her chest.

"Porn? Really?"

"Research, actually. The cinematic output of one Walter Oakley, D.Phil."

"What did he study—*Boobology*?"

"American subcultures, cults, and extended family sects."

"And you just, what, borrowed his work?"

"I digitized the collection for the University and, yes, I kept a copy." His explanation was adequate, and she minimized the video again.

"Not surprising that Oakley became obsessed with the project," he joked, hoping she would take it lightly.

"So what *is* 'C of K'?" She ran her hands across his shoulders, then up into his dark hair. "Hmm?"

"It's…a script I'm working on. For a reality series." Andy leaned back, tried to capture her. She tugged on his curls, but resisted his embrace.

"So *not* the blog you'd get *paid* for." Julia released him. "Have you refreshed your resume? "Like you promised?"

"Hey, easy—I'll get to it."

She picked up the script he had just finished printing, flipping open the cover.

"*Cannibals of Kentucky*? Are you joking?"

It seemed to be the common reaction.

[Reel 17, August 1985; audio only]

(WO) Can you show me your teeth?

(LA) Why.

(WO) Is that blood on your teeth?

(LA) I brush my teeth—

(WO) It may be a symptom of scurvy. Fascinating! Do you ever eat fresh fruit, like oranges?

(LA, after a pause) I eat *meat*.

(WO) Are any of your teeth loose?

(LA) *No*. Don't y'all eat meat?

Burt was somewhat more supportive of his client.

"What do I wear?" Andy asked, desperate for advice.

"I'm your agent—not Queer Eye." There was silence on the line, then Burt relented.

"Let's see… Whatever you have in mind, it's probably *not* right for Boris Petronowa's party. Is it dinner?"

"I…don't think so."

"Then make it as simple as possible—denim without holes, a button-down shirt, but casual—no necktie. A necktie is a sign of submission."

"This is a good thing, right?" Andy pleaded. "I mean, I was hoping to go to his office—"

"Security didn't throw you out, either. You did all right, kid."

Andy had only a moment to bask in Burt's praise before the agent spoke again.

"You say there was a tall blonde in the elevator with Petronowa?"

"She got on—I'm not sure she was *with* him—"

"Did she smile?"

"No, she looked…"

"Predatory. It was Levka, definitely. The power behind the throne. Watch out for her. You didn't *say* anything to her, I hope?"

"No, why?"

"She may *appear* to just be another exccutive in his production company, but remember this: she may not make Petronowa's decisions, but she can *unmake* them. Yeah, it's a dog-eat-dog business."

Andy could only see a bright future unfolding.

"Oh—and one more thing…"

"What's that?"

"Don't drive—hire a car."

"Why?"

"I've seen your car."

[Reel 20, September 1985]

A motel room, shabby, and probably the scientist's. The camera is across the room, on a tripod, or perched on a piece of furniture. Oakley is half-turned towards Laurel Anne, the pair seated on a dingy couch. She is wearing a summer dress, legs crossed, studying her strapped heels. The outfit looks new.

(LA) I'm looking forward to California—there are lots of young people there, aren't there. Going to Hollywood, where y'all make the movies.

(WO) You promised to tell me more. Would you call yourself a priestess?

(LA, bored) I understand the old ways, yeah.

She lifts her breasts, squirming.

(LA) Why do y'all want me to wear this thing?

She tugs on the bra straps.

(WO) Tell me about the old ways, Laurel Anne.

(LA) You already know!

She tosses back her heavy hair and laughs, leaning towards him to plant a kiss on his cheek.

(WO, stammers) So sex is part of your ceremony.

(LA) The young eat the old—eat their

food, then when they die, use up their money. But it doesn't *have* to be that way. The old can eat the young—eat their vigor, eat their *youth*…

Weaving up into the foothills, the hired car took Andy as far as the gate. The Santa Monica Mountains were a dark contrast to the light and noise of human activity in the assemblage of glass and steel cubes perched on the hillside.

The engraved card he had received from Petronowa's officious admin took him past security. He walked up the crushed rock driveway, stepping aside for the limos purring up to deposit their cargo at the door. The evening was pleasantly cool, compared to the city.

Andy lingered outside, admiring the brutal, lavish design, the geometry of light. A pool reflected a topiary garden with a wandering walk framing the property. The mansion was a tight fit for the land, but most of the Trousdale Estates homes were on even smaller lots.

"What do you think?"

Andy turned at the friendly tone of a woman's voice.

"I'd hate to pay the taxes," he replied, studying the speaker. She seemed familiar, but Andy couldn't place her.

"I'm Jill." She was middle-aged, auburn hair trimmed close around her face, dressed simply but elegantly. Jill smiled encouragingly at him as one might a shy animal or small child.

"But it's…nice," he continued. "Seems to have a little more privacy than some of the bigger places."

"Yes, Boris bought the neighboring property and tore down a landmark. Gave some realtors pause."

Jill waited patiently.

"Oh—I'm Andy," he finally supplied, offering his hand. "Sorry, if I seem distracted—I've just got a lot riding on tonight…"

"Would you like to step inside and get a drink, Andy?" she asked. "I'll protect you."

Andy made a show of striding manfully up the walk. If Jill suspected he was shy, she was right.

"I think we were supposed to meet,"

she suggested, leading him into the foyer.

Water flowed through the house in an open channel to the reflecting pool they had passed. Moving through, they stepped out again onto a large patio in several levels on the side of the hill. A full bar had been set up outside, along with a lavish spread of finger food.

"You mean, like fated?" Andy asked, trying to get the attention of the bartender. Jill made an irritated noise, and ordered for them both.

"No—I mean it's totally like Boris to not bother with details like names, or introductions."

Music drifted below the cross-currents of conversations, and Andy saw a string quartet playing to the side. Jill accepted a martini and handed him another.

Awareness dawned. Andy peered at her. "Professor…Neumann?"

"Just call me Jill." It was her turn to frown in recognition. "Are you at UCLA?"

"Well, I took some classes in the graduate program, did some…work…there."

"I thought you looked familiar," she remarked. "And your field is anthropophagy, I take it."

Andy sipped the drink, taking time to parse the word before replying.

"I wouldn't call it my *field*, exactly. But lately, yes, I've been doing some research, revisiting some earlier work, you might say."

Jill seemed amused. "And it occurred

to you it might make for entertaining programming? I don't think there's much appetite for another *Manhunter*."

They made their way through the milling guests and into a quieter corner of the patio. The lights of Beverly Hills were spread out before them in the summer evening. The academic motioned towards a pair of patio chairs, and Andy trailed obediently behind her. They settled down.

"Well, there's no crime or horror, per se," Andy pointed out.

"At least not in the pilot." Jill sighed. "You haven't gotten any management input yet. Not that it isn't an interesting topic, if a bit marginal."

"There are cooking shows, and survival shows..."

She grimaced. "However, this story line is beyond belief."

"So that would make you, what—a cannibal-denier?" Andy assumed a confident slouch as the martini worked on him.

"Not at all," she retorted. "It certainly occurs among humans *in extremis*. And for ceremonial purposes—magical reasoning…"

Andy's attention drifted from the impromptu lecture to the guests around him: directors, actors, media influencers, some he had followed online. The rest, he presumed, were involved in production—or wannabes, like himself.

"So, Jill," he interrupted. "What's a nice scientist like you…"

She finished his thought. "Doing at a producer's party? I work for his production company as a consultant—cultural sensitivity issues."

She waggled a skewered olive at him before popping it into her mouth, nodding to herself. "That's right—I enable a straight white man to make a fortune telling the stories of brown, female, and gay people. *And* avoid being charged with 'cultural misappropriation'."

"How *does* he navigate it? Everybody's *some* group, nobody's *all* groups."

"In a word: sensitivity," Jill replied. "I review the work, call them out on casting, or stereotypes." She shrugged. "Mostly I make sure that hiring is fair and the scripts aren't *too* silly."

Andy sipped. "How do you feel about cannibals as a vulnerable minority?"

She pursed her lips. "I haven't had time for a thorough reading of your script, but"—she grinned— "perhaps we can use the practice as a bridge between different cultures, rather than the PC interpretation of oppressor versus oppressed, colonizer versus native…"

He bit back *Eat or be eaten*, and nodded encouragement.

Jill could make or break his project.

"This would be almost a religious practice," he suggested.

Jill agreed. "The ceremonial consumption of flesh and blood, imbuing the recipient with the donor's qualities, or powers—"

"Don't forget semen," said a sultry voice behind Andy.

He started, splashing himself with gin, and turned to find the tall figure of Levka looming behind him. The hand resting possessively upon his shoulder was so light that he had not felt its presence.

Levka wore what Andy thought at first was a black pantsuit. The fabric, however, was sheer enough for lingerie pajamas, merely shadowing her form. Her bright hair was gathered into a plait wrapped around her head.

The executive continued, "You'll find that more semen is consumed in Hollywood than human flesh and blood combined, and for the same reason."

She sipped what might have been an Old Fashioned, a large cherry as unnaturally red as her full lips bobbing in its depths.

"Which is?" Jill prompted.

The blonde leaned down between them.

"*Power*," she murmured.

Jill laughed lightly, and Andy, convinced it was prudent not to comment, merely chuckled.

"Haven't you grilled our guest enough?" Levka purred. "He looks ready to be served up."

Andy tried to place her voice. It could have belonged to a glamorous movie star of the mid-twentieth century, all whiskey and cigarettes crossing ruby lips, a trace of

Southern drawl.

"We're almost done," Jill hinted. "Why don't you run along and tell Boris that Andy's here?"

The executive brought her mouth to Jill's ear, whispering something, then kissing her on the cheek. Straightening, she glanced at Andy with a slight smile and strolled away.

He admired her retreat, wondering in a vague, alcohol-infused way where he'd seen her, until Jill cleared her throat.

"Levka is quite successful at what she does."

"Which is?"

"Survival. It's a very competitive business." Jill frowned into her empty glass, then leaned over to examine his.

"I see we need a refresh. But just one more question."

"Of course."

"When you were in the department, did you ever come across the work of a Walter Oakley? He was interested in American folk legends and cult behavior, especially in the American South."

Andy frowned, as if searching his memory, while desperately crafting a reply.

"Oakley? Did he publish in this field? I don't think I came across any papers…" It was conveniently true.

"No, in fact, he worked in the 80's. Didn't publish much before he…vanished."

"You don't say?" Andy tried to avoid overacting. "I'll have to make a note to look him up." He took out his phone as if to take a memo. "Where did you say Oakley did his field work?"

"I didn't." Jill waved it away. "Don't bother; Oakley didn't amount to much. But…as it happens, it was Kentucky."

Andy felt her watching him.

"That's where your story's set, isn't it?" she asked.

Andy nodded, appearing thoughtful. "You know, I do recall his name—nothing published, just some files in the department."

"That would be him, better at collecting data than disseminating it." Jill stood, offering her arm. "And then he just vanished from Kentucky."

"Maybe Oakley was eaten by

a…mountain lion," Andy suggested.

With a cinematic flourish, Andy interlaced his arm in hers, and they strolled back towards the bar.

"Ever been to Kentucky?" She asked him.

"Uh, no—never had the chance."

"Too bad—I thought you might be able to suggest some targets for location scouting. Usually a scriptwriter has some vision of the setting, even if he's smart enough not to belabor the script with the details." She smiled encouragement.

Andy felt his heart pound. "Oh, I *do* have some ideas…" He summoned up a few of the town names he could recall from Oakley's mind-numbing monologues to season his lie.

"Well, good," Jill said peremptorily, leading him into the glass cubes to join the shambling herd of guests, their conversations and laughter.

"Boris will be pleased."

Jill was offering her opinion to the producer in a sidebar, just out of earshot. Boris was nodding, with an occasional sidelong glance at the would-be screenwriter. Andy feigned interest in his refreshed drink while straining to hear, but soon became absorbed in identifying as many celebrities as he could. Julie wouldn't believe him—if she ever spoke to him again, for failing to extend the invitation to her. He wanted to take out his phone and post a few pictures, but thought it would make him appear a *wannabe*.

Then all of that activity seemed like background for one person, gliding slowly through the crowd. Wherever she went, frivolity was dampened, and deference appeared.

Levka moved like a great cat through their midst. Watching guests defer to her, Andy was reminded of small animals, rolling over before the predator—whether feigning death or preparing for it. The filmy pantsuit revealed her rolling hips, and Andy felt some familiar response harden him. He wondered what it would be like to roll over for *her*, supine, defenseless…

As if listening, she turned, and locked eyes with him, for a moment, displaying that sly trace of a smile, so familiar…

"Andy?" Boris rumbled, then—perhaps noticing the object of his abstraction—grinned and took him by the arm.

"Come; we should talk. Plenty of time for fun later."

Jill appeared subdued, and seeing him in Boris's orbit, drained her drink.

"I think Andy and I need an update," she suggested, moving to intercept them.

Boris laughed. "You can have what's left of him when Levka's through; right now, we have business." He turned to Andy.

"I realize I haven't been a very good host." With that, the producer steered him away from Jill and Levka and the glitterati, and deeper into the sterile steel and glass warren. "I should show you the place."

Andy glanced back to nod at the scientist, who turned away, frowning.

They made a circuit of the ground level, past lavish bedrooms, pristine baths, an impressive study.

"Why don't you let me make it up to you. Hungry? I'm hungry—why don't you stay for dinner?" Boris grinned. "I assume you're free?"

Andy nodded, convinced he had just won a victory, of sorts.

"Let's see where the important work gets done," Boris suggested.

Andy decided to press his advantage.

"Location testing—I have some ideas I'd like to share…"

They approached the burnished steel

door of an elevator, and Boris waved his phone at a featureless panel. The door slid open silently, and they stepped inside.

"All business, eh? I suppose you have some casting tips, too?" He chuckled.

"Some ideas for *Laurel Anne*, I suppose?" He grew serious. "The *Laurel Annes* of the world are *my* job."

The elevator descended.

"Of course," Andy deferred. "Just where *are* we going? Didn't I see the kitchen upstairs?"

"The home kitchen, yes—very elegant, connected appliances and all that rot. I thought you'd like to see where the *real* cooking goes on for an event like this."

The younger man couldn't understand why he *would* be interested but wasn't about to say that.

"Real cooking?" he repeated.

"The banquet kitchen."

The door slid open, and they faced a spacious tiled chamber full of gleaming metal counters, cooking hoods over expansive grills, and multiple large ovens.

"I'm very proud of this place—we can take on any meal for any number. Tonight, for example—ribs for one hundred guests, give or take a few leaf-eaters."

He laughed, shambling down the long row of cooking stations, a finger gliding along the stainless steel surface. Andy followed.

"Why is no one here?"

"Crew's on break—dinner is all prepared, waiting for us upstairs. The staff is eating now, so they can be ready to serve—"

His phone chimed, and he nodded.

"—in exactly one-half hour."

An impressive array of polished knives, cleavers and saws, filled a rack on the back wall, above a broad oak table.

"I talked to my people—Jill, Levka, others." Boris's arm fell heavily across Andy's shoulders.

"Nothing personal, but they just don't think you're *hungry* enough to make it in Hollywood. Levka, now, came out here with nothing, changed her name, and clawed her way to the top. My muse, my lioness…"

Boris squeezed Andy's shoulder. "Do you work out? Feels like you work out.

Muscular."

He motioned at another steel door, guiding Andy forward as the young man struggled with a response. Petronowa waved his phone again. The door gave a solid click, swinging open.

"Walk-in freezer. Come in; I want to show you the secret of fine dining."

The producer entered, toggling on the lights, Andy trailing behind.

"Can you guess the answer?" Boris ushered him forward, stepping aside.

The young man shuddered in the cold, facing a row of hanging carcasses.

"No—what?"

Boris grinned. "The *ingredients*— always, fresh ingredients. See?"

As Andy stared around at the pale,

cold flesh, racks of ribs, hanging hocks, the door slammed behind him, and the light was extinguished. Alone in the darkness, he fumbled for a handle, and finding none, pounded on the door until his fist ached.

Crouched in the freezing cold, Andy recalled a sultry voice, and it came to him, how he'd encountered Levka before. He found he had lost his appetite.

First published in *The J J. Outre Review*, Dark Passages Publishing, 2019

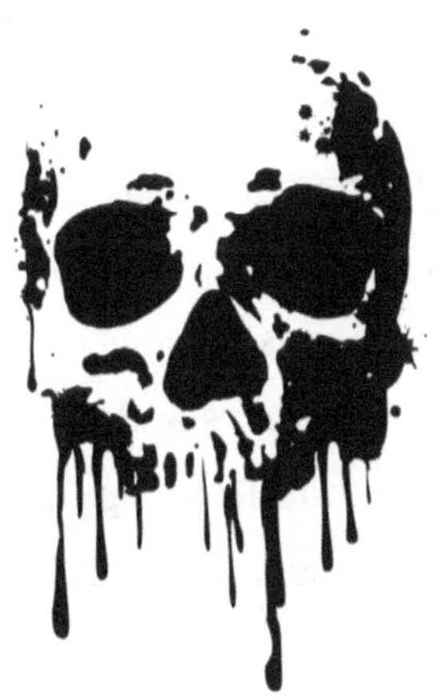

HALLOWEEN PUB NIGHT

By D.M. Burdett

I leave the pub, yell a drunken *Goodbye*, and head home.

From Mrs Orton's porch, a pumpkin

mouths its flame-coloured scream. Beer-filled me decides I want it. I sneak in the gate—a giggling child—can't wait to show the guys my prize.

As my hands reach out, the door opens. Mrs Orton stands there in her nightdress, toothless gummy smile wrinkling her face. "Tut-tut," she sneers. With a flick of her wrist, my world fades to black.

***

A year goes by before I see my friends. I call from Mrs Orton's porch, but they don't hear my flame-coloured scream.

REINVENTING THE NIGHT

By Jacqueline Moran Meyer

"I can see the entrance from here. You brought your ID, right?"

My heart races momentarily. I pat the back pocket of my Jordache jeans, and to my relief, I feel the familiar rectangular shape. "Yep. Duh."

The bouncer, whom I dub Thor, checks everyone's identification. His flashlight sweeps from ID to face while he makes his snap decisions--yea or nay. Depending on some internal algorithm, Thor either hands the credentials back to the rejected as he shakes his head or rips up the offending cards until they resemble mulch. He points his muscled index finger toward the parking lot, banishing those losers to the elements or back to hearth and home. Oh, the power a bouncer wields. His rapid-fire decisions change fate.

"Should we start bleating?" I ask,

looking at the winding double line leading up to the door.

We inch forward, a herd of strays, heading to slaughter. The strangers' bodies shield my small frame from the bitter wind coming off the bay adjacent to the abandoned warehouse turned club, home to our destination: The Golden Leaf.

I nudge my sister, holding the license in front of her face. She tilts her head up and squints. Maureen looks warm in her black-and-neon-green down ski jacket, while I shiver.

"I'm a year older than you," I tease.

"Oh, Jesus, Peg! You didn't bring *that* ID again, did you? I may just kill you if they don't let us in."

"Not funny. You'd never hurt me. I'm

all you've got, whether you like it or not. What kind of guardian brings their young ward out to the bar?" I joke.

"You need to stop reading *Jane Eyre*. You're so dramatic. I know you're all I've got. I miss Mom, too."

Our beautiful, loving mom, Mary, died last year. We do not like to speak about her murder. She left us with our father, neither fit nor able to be a parent. By some form of divine intervention, my sister convinced the court she could be my guardian until I turned eighteen and finished high school. Maureen may be only twenty-two, but I feel safer with her than I do with anyone else in the world. We share blood, history, and many secrets.

I stare at the well-worn stolen ID in my

hand and convince myself Thor will let me in.

"I don't think it's so bad. Tonight, I'm Theresa d'Ascoli, five-seven, brown hair and eyes, born January 22, 1968. Twenty years old last Friday. Happy birthday to me—the Theresa me."

"Let's hope he needs glasses and has zero sense of scale. You're five feet and have red hair and blue eyes, and you're only seventeen. My God, you've got a drawer filled with licenses. At least read the damn thing before you put it in your pocket."

"Don't worry, Sis. Thor lets in any human with a working vagina. The only underage-looking guys who get in look rich and preppy."

"You and your nicknames for people. His name could be Thor, though."

I love amusing Maureen.

"He'll let me in because I'm a chick. One of the only great things about being a girl—you get into bars."

"You think being able to waltz into a bar, underage, drinking until you're shit-faced, and getting preyed upon is the greatest thing about being a woman?"

"Yes. And ladies drink for free tonight. Maybe we'll meet someone to make Mom proud. We'll use our magic powers to take the form of any man's fantasy. Right, Sis?" I wink at her to punctuate my remark.

Maureen and I lean on each other, and she opens her arms to hug me and keep me warm.

When we reach Thor, he flashes his light on my sister's legal ID and her face before waving her through. He does the same with me but, in a thick Long Island accent, adds "Make it betta next time, sweetheart."

With her hat and coat off, Maureen waits for me inside. We don't look like sisters or even friends, but we are both. Tall, thin, calm and collected, Maureen is told she resembles actress Ali McGraw. In contrast, I resemble Laura Ingalls, from *Little House on the Prairie*. Unfair.

We push through a long, dark hallway in a cresting wave of neon earrings, Members Only jackets, perms, and hairspray until confronting a rickety metal staircase spiraling to unknown depths below. Descending, we pass people smoking, couples swapping spit, druggies snorting cocaine, and the occasional comatose-looking partiers being dragged up the stairs by friends, fighting through the tsunami of youth in a vain attempt to get them out of the building.

The sound of New Wave music gets louder. The traffic on the stairs starts and stops until we reach the bottom. We walk through a doorway into an enormous, windowless basement. It takes us a few minutes to adjust our eyes and ears to the onslaught of flashing lights, deafening music, and bright clothing. Three bars line the perimeter of the main room, with a large dance floor in the center.

We order gin and tonics at the first bar

we can reach.

"Cheers! To our first cups of courage," Maureen says.

We inhale the drinks and head straight to the dance floor.

About half an hour later, two young men, double-fisting beers and wearing identical blue Brooks Brothers suits, saunter over to us while we're dancing to Rick Astley's "Never Gonna Give You Up." Maureen selects Brooks #1, the better-looking one, of course. Therefore, plump Brooks #2 becomes mine, and we start screaming at each other in a semi-futile attempt to make conversation.

When he dances away from me, I can still see his lips moving, but I only hear the music. When he gyrates back in my direction, I catch snippets of what he's saying before he spins and wriggles away again.

"Hey, little girl. My name's—"

We've known each other for so long / Your heart's been aching.

"I make more money in a year than my dad did his whole—"

We know the game, and we're gonna play it.

"Golfing and models. I bought a boat last week with a—"

Don't tell me you're too blind to see—

"Wall Street, baby. The only women who work there are bitch—"

Never gonna give you up / Never gonna let you down.

"I bought a red Beemer and—"

Never gonna make you cry / Never gonna say goodbye.

Brooks #2 is slurring every word. He doesn't ask me anything until he's finished the two beers he's been spilling all over himself and the floor.

"Will you steal me a drink, Sweetie? It's ladies' night. You get drinks for free," he screams in my ear, explaining how ladies' nights work, as if I don't already know.

I stop dancing and stand as still as a statue. Brooks #2 continues chattering about himself until he realizes I'm not moving. I smile and wiggle my finger in a "come hither young man" motion. He struts over and leans in close for a kiss. I turn my head to scream in his ear, "Buy it yourself,

Beemer."

Unfazed, he dances away to find another young thing to listen to him and supply him with free drinks.

Brooks #2's drunkenness triggers me. Visions of my father flash through my mind. Dad often came home looking so handsome in his fedora, carrying the remnants of a long day at work and the effects of the bar car into the house with him. Along with his scratchy face, the smell of cigarettes and beer would greet us at the front door.

Always angry. It was only years later that I recognized the cause of his behavior—alcohol. When the time came for Maureen and me to go to bed, our parents ate dinner alone. Uncertainty about how the rest of the night would unfold filled me with anxiety. Most nights consisted of violence towards Mom. Maureen and I also became our father's targets.

The best nights were the ones when our dad didn't come home at all. It puzzled me why Mom got so upset when this happened. When he wasn't home, I never worried about him hurting any of us.

Maureen is laughing with Brooks #1. She winks at me in acknowledgment when I motion to her and pretend to guzzle from a bottle and point to the bar.

While ordering a gin and tonic, I lock eyes with guy in a pink polo shirt across the bar.

He is next to me in a flash, and we

make small talk. After about five minutes, his tone changes.

"My God, you're way too young to be here."

"No, I'm not."

"Yes, you are. Go home. There are so many creepy men in here. Bars aren't safe," Pink Polo says.

"Why are *you* here?" I ask.

"Maybe I'm a bad guy, or maybe I'm just a twenty-four-year-old out with his friends after bowling and dinner. Are you alone?"

"No. My sister's over there."

His friends stand next to him now. I hadn't seen them walk over.

"Guys, we should drive her home or call her a cab. She can't be more than fourteen." He glances at me. "No offense."

My eyes tear up, and I'm not sure why. Do I believe Pink Polo cares about my safety? No. Is he condescending? Yes. Could he be a bad guy and worthy of my wrath? Yes. Do I look like I'm fourteen years old? Damn him!

"You're making the little girl sad, man," one of his stoner friends remarks.

"Stop," I say, and I spin on my heels to walk away.

"Be careful," Pink Polo shouts at my back.

A man, whose eyes have followed me all night, stands near the bar. The stranger's face would be handsome if not for his pockmarked skin and close-set eyes. He is standing alone, and he is looking at me. I think this may be the one, or Pink Polo, who is still staring at me from across the room. I'm feeling the effects of the alcohol, and those plastic cups of courage give me the nerve I need to walk over and confront him.

"Hi. Do I know you?"

"You do now. Where's your friend?" he asks.

"My sister? She's dancing. You're watching me. Why?" I ask, pretending I don't know what he is thinking.

"You're gorgeous. I can't stop staring."

His voice drips with an almost convincing charm. I pretend to be shy by looking at the floor, but in my head, I'm projectile vomiting all over his shirt.

"Were those jerks bothering you? You looked scared."

"No. Well, I'm not sure."

"I think you need a drink."

"No. I'm fine."

"Just one beer." He orders a Budweiser without asking if I like beer.

"So, what do you do?" I ask, since he doesn't seem interested in introductions and exchanging names.

He scowls, appearing annoyed at the question, and hesitates before answering.

"I'm a lawyer. I've been in this suit since six-thirty this morning," he lies.

"Impressive," I lie in return.

His hands are tanned and calloused. They aren't the hands of a man who works in an office. They belong to a man who labors outdoors. Construction or garbage collection, maybe. His cheap clothes are far too big for him, which is astonishing since he's a big guy, at least six-two. The suit looks like an off-the-rack Sears special, I decide. And presto—I dub him Sears.

The way a man wears a suit says a lot about him. Despite his faults, my dad can rock a suit. He buys only the best, although he cannot wear one at the moment. Dad looks so confident in a suit; he could play baseball in a tux and look natural.

Sears isn't as good at faking it. He reminds me of how my cousin Billy looked in the suit he wore to my mother's funeral. Billy moved around the funeral home stiffly. Sears is doing the same thing, and when he leans over to grab the bottles from the bartender, I see that the white, X-shaped thread holding the vent flap closed in the back is still intact. He doesn't realize he is supposed to remove it.

I take the beer. "Thank you."

"How old are you?"

"Twenty," I lie.

He smirks but sips his drink instead of commenting. "Do you want to go to a party?" he asks.

What nerve.

"No, thanks. I gotta go home."

"Yeah. I should do the same. Can I have your number?"

I pull a pen and an old receipt out of my pocket and write down "Tracy," with a fake number.

"I'm going to find my sister and go

home. Good night." I hand him the receipt. He winks.

Pink Polo had stared in my direction for the duration of my exchange with Sears. I glance at him from the corner of my eye as I walk toward Maureen, who is still flirting with Brooks #1.

"I'm going to walk home," I say.

She raises her eyebrows and looks around to see if I am with anyone. "Are you sure, Peg?"

"One hundred percent. I realize this isn't the usual plan, but I want to walk. You can stay here with Brooks #1."

"Who is Brooks #1?" Brooks #1 asks.

"They do have names, you know. Be fierce, Sis," Maureen says, laughing.

"I'll see you later."

As I leave the bar and the cold air hits my face, I feel free and sober. After a few minutes of walking, headlights shine on me from behind, casting my body's long shadow on the sidewalk. The car isn't passing and slows down as it approaches. I walk faster, keeping my head down and resisting the urge to turn around. The old car hovers beside me.

I glance over at a banged-up Camaro. The black-tinted windows conceal the faces of anyone inside. The bass thumps so heavily that the concrete vibrates beneath my feet. I am certain the driver is someone from the bar. My guess: Pink Polo and his friends. The passenger-side window begins to roll down, and the music stops.

"Tracy, what are you doing?" Sears

calls to me.

"Hi. I'm fine," I say, and I walk a little faster, still keeping my head down.

"My car is nice and warm. You must be freezing out there. I'll drive you home. Trust me—I'm harmless."

"No, thanks. I live just a few blocks away; I'll manage."

"You aren't wearing a warm coat. Who let you leave the house?"

*I can wear whatever the hell I want.*I stop, pivot, and glare at him through the window as he brings the car to a stop.

"I understand. Don't accept rides from strangers, blah, blah, blah. I'll follow until I know you're home."

OK. Sears will not take no for an answer, and I'm convinced he is not going to leave me alone. I decide to accept the ride. In my head, I'm singing, "I'm scared; I'm scared; I'm scared." But I'm not scared.

"OK. Fine. Thank you."

I try to open the passenger-side door but can't. *Worrisome*. He skips out and around the front of his car and uses a key to unlock it.

"After you, Princess."

He grips the back of my head, pushing me down into the seat, then slams the door. He walks around the front, scowling and muttering to himself while he settles in behind the steering wheel.

"Only a few blocks away. Turn left on Driftwood Drive," I say.

He doesn't respond.

He passes Driftwood Drive, and I can sense the natural evil in control of this car.

"Oh…you missed my turn…easy to do. We can turn around in any driveway… Oh, I see an easy one to turn around in…"

I'm speaking too fast, and I sound panicky. Sears grips the steering wheel with one hand and runs the calloused fingers of the other through his hair. No more words are spoken until we reach the bridge.

He is taking me to the beach. I stare out the window and realize I recognize this place.

My family used to come here when Maureen and I were little and somewhat happy. But the bad memories outweigh the good ones. Our parents constantly fought toward the end. At night, we would press our ears against our bedroom door, straining to listen to their conversation once the screaming turned to whispers. A month before our mom died, we heard snippets of a terrible conversation.

"I'll kill you all if you leave me, Mary. I will. The girls will be first, and I'll make you watch. I'll kill you and myself. I love you. Don't make me do it."

This terrified Maureen and me.

One night, my mom let us sleep over at separate friends' houses. Mom gave us each a big hug before we left. Dad never allowed us to go anywhere. If Dad knew our whereabouts and tried to find us, Maureen and I wouldn't be here now.

When I returned home early the next

morning, yellow crime tape, police officers, and a hysterical Maureen greeted me.

Maureen screamed, "Mom's gone forever, Peg! Dad is, too, the bastard. I hope he dies of old age on death row or gets a needle in the arm to finish him off."

The vile words spewing from Sears's thin lips bring me back to the present moment. It won't be long until we drive over the second bridge leading to the ocean.

I manage to tune Sears out, and my thoughts return to Maureen. After the murder, Maureen and I visited various psychic mediums in a futile attempt to contact our mom. One psychic referred us to her witch friend.

"Eva is the real deal. For a price, she will grant you one wish; just be careful how you phrase it."

We went into the city to visit Eva, a tall and striking young blonde. She looked more like a Coppertone model than a vessel of vengeance. She didn't live in a grimy back-alley apartment. Instead, Eva lived in a luxury prewar apartment on Park Avenue, with fifteen-foot ceilings and sleek, modern furniture.

"What is your wish?" Eva asked in a bored voice after we handed her a hundred-dollar bill.

"We want to rid the world of people like our father," Maureen said.

"And I want them to be terrified before they are gone," I added.

Sears's touch jolts me back to the present. He strokes my hair with his calloused hands. I keep my back turned to him and shift closer to the window. Now I'm paying much more attention to what he is saying.

"You're so fucking stupid to accept a ride from a stranger, but I won't be a stranger for long. You're so dumb. A stupid moron."

"Did I tell you my dad is a police officer?" I do not turn to face him.

"You're lying," he says with a little less bravado. "Which precinct?"

"Michael Fitzpatrick. Deer Park, 108th Precinct."

"You're not a good liar. Too late now, anyway. I bet your dad will be relieved to be rid of you—his stupid whore daughter.”

"I'm not lying.”

"You know what, Princess? It's cold tonight. I can take off all your clothes and leave you on this empty beach to die.”

We're over the second bridge and traveling down a sandy road. I don't move as Sears proceeds to spew evil in my direction.

"Every year, they find a body or two out here. And I know who puts them there.”

"Why are you trying to scare me?" I turn to face him. My eyes are clear and dry. I am angry.

"Don't you believe me? Do I scare you? I usually have you stupid girls blubbering now.”

"I'm glad I told my sister to write

down your license plate number before I left," I lie.

"Impossible," he laughs.

"OK. I'm lying, but Maureen took your wallet, asshole."

A half-truth. Maureen didn't take his wallet—I did, and it is in my jacket pocket. I pinched it when he reached over the bar to order drinks. Pickpocketing is a compulsion of mine--one I am not proud of, but it can be useful. My collection of wallets includes people from all walks of life.

He checks his back pocket with one hand and shoots me a terrifying, dead-eyed stare. He is screaming obscenities now, waving one arm about and shouting about all the demented things he's going to do to me. I turn around again and look out the window as he pulls off the road and heads down a narrow, secluded path just wide enough for his car. After a few minutes of driving, the car lurches to a stop.

"You ruined everything. Maybe your sister is still there. I can go back and snatch her after I'm finished with you."

He reacts to my shoulders moving up and down and says, "Thank you! Finally, some tears."

I try to open the car door although I know I won't be able to.

"The door is locked. You're trapped in here with me, Princess."

We sit there, his eyes boring into the back of my head as my shoulders continue to heave.

"Yes, you should be crying. You deserve this." He grabs my hair and yanks my head around to face him.

Confusion washes over his face when he realizes I'm not crying. I'm laughing.

Staring at my face, he releases his grip on my hair and starts hollering. His eyes bug out of his skull cartoonishly.

"Don't touch me! What…are you?"

He screams and claws at the door handle, but I pin him down with my knees and place my rotting hands around his neck.

He cannot stop shrieking.

"You aren't real! Please, get away from me. Stop!" Sears begs.

I turn my head to see my transformation in the rearview mirror. Oh,

I *am* hideous. I'm always a little surprised by what I look like, because my appearance is never the same in these situations, but nothing scares me anymore. I am unrecognizable. My bloated face is mottled—red and purple. My lips are split and broken, with puss-oozing sores. And the pièce de résistance is the army of maggots marching out of my nose.

"Wow, Sears, you are a twisted one."

I gape at him with a grotesque smile. He wails and pleads for mercy.

"Am I still your princess?" I demand. "Scream and cry all you want. Have I turned into your biggest fear? You made me like this, Sears. I've turned into the thing you sick, evil people fear the most."

What I am about to do never gets less

satisfying.

"I'd like a little mood music," I say over his screams.

Careful to keep him immobile, I reach around and turn on the radio.

"Perfect!" I squeal, as George Michael's song *Faith* streams through the car's stereo.

"I love this song. *Baby, I know you're asking me to stay / Say 'Please, please don't go away.'*"

While I sing, my hands tighten around Sears's neck, and I strangle him into unconsciousness. I wait for him to come to, patting his face occasionally and cooing to him to hasten the process.

When he awakens, I do it all again. And again. And again. I am patient. I enjoy it when his eyes flutter open and he starts to scream. When I can no longer revive him, my mission is complete. It never gets old.

I toss his body in the trunk before transforming back into my wholesome, youthful exterior. Glad to be the one left alive in the car, I drive back over the bridge to Maureen. The sky is clear, the stars are shining, and there is one less Sears in the world to hurt people.

***

I find our Buick about a block away from The Golden Leaf and park behind it. We don't live around here. Every Saturday night, Maureen and I pick a new hunting ground. We change our looks a little every time. We don't always go to bars, though. Sometimes we go into the city and walk the desolate streets or wait at a bus stop late at night, looking for predators and killers.

Maureen gets out of our car and walks toward me. I step out of the car and unlock the passenger-side door with a key on Sears's keyring.

"Everything went OK?" Maureen asks.

"Yep. The door won't open without this." I show Maureen the key.

"Clever," Maureen says. She rolls her eyes and hops into the passenger seat.

We speak when I am settled behind the wheel.

"You were gone a long time, Peg. I'm

tired, and I want to go to sleep. I wish you'd stop playing with them before you kill them. A little sick, don't you think? And you take forever."

"You do it your way, and I'll do it mine. He's still in the trunk, by the way. We should dump him and the car somewhere and torch it. I read that the police use a new DNA-evidence thingy now. We can't be too careful."

"Let's sit for a minute. It would be so much easier if we could make it look like the ass was in an altercation; we could leave him here. Evidence of some kind of bar fight would be enough. We could wipe down your prints, or something," Maureen suggests.

"How was the rest of your night?" I

ask.

"Brooks #1 was a bust. He was a decent guy. I am either losing my touch or finding nice guys on purpose. I almost felt like I was on a proper date tonight. Don't get me wrong; I know we're doing something good."

"How'd it end?"

"He drove me home," she said, putting "home" in air quotes. "I picked some random-ass house. He asked if he could kiss me on the cheek, and I said, "Sure." I gave him a fake name and number, and I walked around the back of the house and waited for him to leave."

"Great. No mistakes. We only kill the bad ones. There are many good ones; always nice to remember. We're doing a good thing."

"Yes," she says.

"I think we should bury him," I say.

"OK. A shovel is in the Buick, right? We can ditch his car off the pier, I guess."

"I hope so. I'm surprised by who's in the trunk. I thought it would be another guy this time. Did you notice the guy I was talking to, wearing the pink polo shirt? I thought for sure it would be him or one of his friends," I say.

"No, I didn't, but I bet you called him Pink Polo in your head all night."

Just as I'm about to respond, I hear a light *tap, tap, tap* at my window. I roll it down a crack.

"Pink Polo?" I ask.

"What?" he replies.

My sister and I take in the activity outside Sears's car. One man, holding a knife, begins to drag it across the passenger-side door. Pink Polo palms a baseball bat, ready to use it at any moment. They all start banging on the windows and trying to open the locked doors. They're howling.

"We're so happy you came back. Get out, ladies. Let's play," Pink Polo says.

Maureen and I look at each other and crack up.

"This is our lucky night," I say, while the bat shatters the back window.

We'll be home a little later than we thought.

First published in *Bewildering Stories #831*, Bewildering Press, 2019

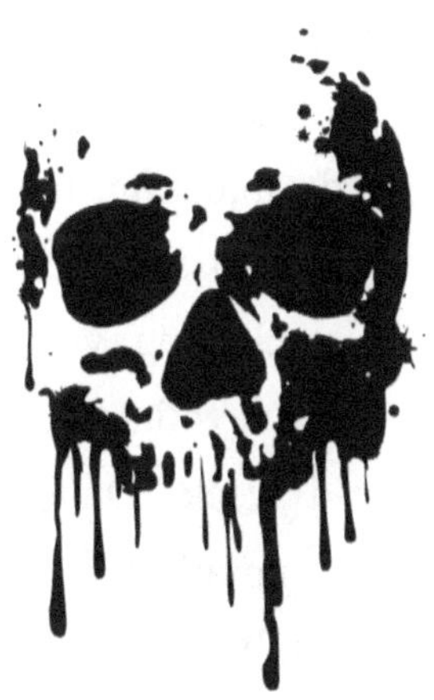

KARMA

By Galina Trefil

Chill, kill, and ill—those were the theories of what extinguished the megafauna, such as the smilodon and the woolly mammoth, 11,000 years ago.

An ice age, mass murder by humans,

or a plague. Which was the culprit?

Perhaps it was a combination, the scientist mused, injecting the specially-designed plague into the fresh cadaver's cold, but soon quickening, veins.

Today, massive climate change had made the world weak. On every corner people were ripping all other life-forms to shreds. Really, only one component was needed to enact another mass extinction…

Humanity has this coming, he thought. Who could possibly argue?

THE BOY

By Jodi Jensen

I couldn't have picked a worse place to break down. My car was older than I was, and with the construction on the freeway, I'd opted for the frontage road instead. Great idea, until it detoured, and I went left when I should've gone right.

And now…

I glanced over my shoulder at the pathetic heap of junk that was my car. Who even knew what the problem was this time? The old rust-bucket had shuddered, sputtered, then died, leaving me stranded in an abandoned industrial area. I didn't bother to try my cell. I already knew it was dead. The stupid thing wouldn't hold a charge for more than an hour and my car was too ancient to have a port to plug it into.

I turned and stared at the road in front of me, desolate except for the lone structure looming in the back corner of a deserted parking lot. Past the building though, the road veered left, back towards the city.

That was where I needed to go if I was going to get some help.

With daylight waning, I slung my purse over my shoulder and started walking. It didn't take long for me to realize my high heels were less than ideal. Every few steps I wobbled as the stilettos got hung up in the pock-marked asphalt. I hadn't taken more than twenty steps before I stopped and slipped the shoes off. Better to go barefoot and have my feet sore than trip, fall, and break my neck.

I shoved the heels into my purse and continued down the road. As I picked my way around small rocks and the odd shard of broken glass, I approached the vast, empty parking lot. The edges were lined with overgrown flower beds, where nothing but dandelions bloomed, and half-dead shrubs cast spidery shadows on the ground. Every few feet there was a break between the bushes that provided glimpses of the eerie warehouse beyond.

Something rustled in the tall weeds behind me, and as I whipped around, my foot came down on a sharp pebble. "Son-of-a-bitch in hell," I muttered, reaching to dislodge the culprit. I'd forgotten all about the noise, until I heard it again. My heart thundered as I squinted into the dusky recesses on the side of the road. It had to be some sort of animal, a stray cat maybe, or a raccoon.

"Get out of here," I shouted. "Go on!"

The rustling came to an abrupt stop.

I gathered my courage and turned back

to the road. I'd only taken a couple steps when the rustling returned with vigor. Out of the corner of my eye, I saw a small figure dart from the shadows and race across the asphalt.

"Wait!" I dropped my purse and took off after the child. "Do you need some help?"

The kid slipped between a gap in the bushes and disappeared into the parking lot.

"Come back!" I barreled through the opening and ran, heedless of the debris beneath my bare feet.

It wasn't until the child reached a broken light pole and stopped to turn and look at me that I realized it was a boy. A very young, very dirty, little boy. He couldn't have been more than eight or nine. His clothes were ragged, his hair an unruly, matted mess that covered half his face.

I slowed to a brisk walk and held out my hand. "Are you okay, kid?"

He backed up a step.

I slowed even further, cautious lest I startle him. "I'm not going to hurt you."

The boy cast a glance at the building behind him.

I followed his gaze and nearly jumped out of my skin as a loud crash reverberated from behind a rusty metal door on the front.

The boy stood still. Too still. Frozen as he stared at the warehouse.

As the last vestiges of evening faded, a chill that had nothing to do with the autumn breeze swept over me. The building, with its peeling paint and broken windows, took on a sinister tinge in the dark, and the young boy took a hesitant step towards it. Then another.

"No, don't—"

The rusted door swung open, revealing an inky blackness so dark it was unnatural.

Every instinct I had screamed at me to leave this place. To run and not look back.

I would have—should have. Except I couldn't.

Not without the boy.

"Kid," I hissed. "Get back here."

He kept walking. His small shoulders rigid, and his tattered shoes squishing with each step he took.

"Stop!" I shouted, desperate to get his attention.

Two more steps and he was at the edge of a sidewalk. A cracked and broken path that led straight into the gaping darkness.

He stopped.

Thank God he stopped.

I hurried towards the boy, intent on getting us both out of here.

As soon as I reached him, he slid his grubby hand in mine and pointed at the building. "Sumpthin's in there," he said in a small, cold voice.

"We don't have to go in." I tried to pull him away but froze as he looked up at me with pitch black eyes.

"You do."

Thick dark vines snaked around my feet and jerked me onto the sidewalk. I screamed and stumbled forwards as more vines sprouted from the cracks, wrapped around my ankles and dragged me closer and closer to the door.

I twisted and fought to get away, only managing a single glimpse of the boy. He stood perfectly still, his black eyes fixed on me, unrepentant.

"No!" I shrieked.

The darkness grabbed me, swallowed me into its gaping emptiness.

A raspy voice echoed as I tumbled into the pitch-black maw.

"Bring me more, boy…"

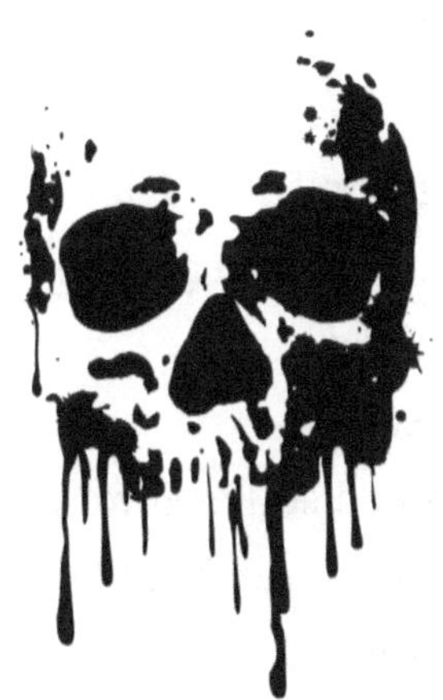

CANDY CORN WOLVES

By Stacey Jaine McIntosh

Candy corn littered the forest floor as wolves raced by. The smell of iron tainted the air.

Blood.

Fear.

Rabbits had long returned to their dens, but not all made it. The mangled corpse of one lay by a gnarled tree.

More blood.

More fear.

Time stood still as if for one night the rest of the world had fallen away.

Perhaps it had.

As the sun slipped above the horizon, bones broke and naked bodies of men and women lay tangled among the sugary treats.

But this was not a trick.

Werewolves roamed here, and not just on Halloween.

First published in *Forest of Fear*, Blood Song Books, 2019

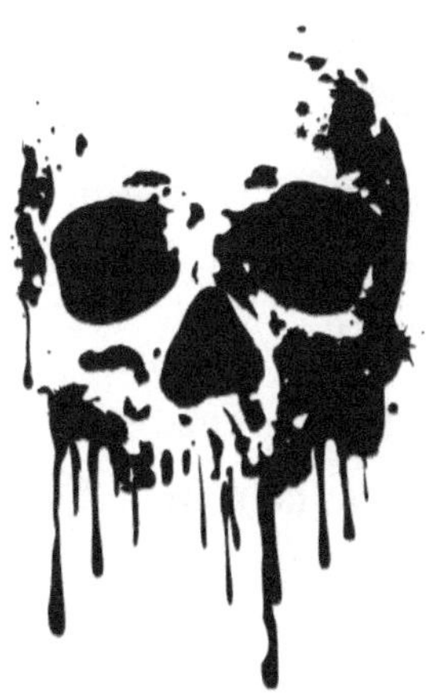

HUNGRY

By Dale Parnell

"It happened again."

"Oh, honey, I'm sorry. Was it the same kind of thing?"

"Yeah, middle of nowhere and I'm being chased by…something; I don't know. I can't see it."

"Maybe you should go to the doctor?"

"And tell him what? I'm a grown man and I've had the same dream for two weeks, that's all."

"They're nightmares Justin, they might be able to do something."

"Like what?"

"I don't know, but something. Look at you; you're exhausted all the time!"

"It'll go away. It's just a stupid dream. Now please, can we just not talk about it?"

"OK, fine. But if it happens again tonight, I'm making an appointment with the doctor."

"Hmm, maybe."

I didn't want to admit it to Karen, but

it was starting to get to me. Two weeks now and every night was the same thing. I'd wake up yelling, kicking out at the sheets - I even caught Karen once. And then I'd lay there, terrified and dripping with sweat. It was ridiculous. I hadn't had bad dreams since I was a kid; who even has bad dreams when they get to my age? But here I was, exhausted all day, barely able to concentrate at work, and honestly, I was starting to get anxious about going to sleep. It was stupid; I never even saw what was chasing me, but deep down I was petrified of what would happen if it ever caught me. I kissed Karen goodnight and rolled over, secretly grateful that she would be reading for a while and that her bedside lamp was on.

***

It's too dark. There should be street lights but none of them are working and it's too dark. It's cold as well. I've got my new coat on, but it's not working properly and I can feel the cold in my guts. I was trying to find the way home, but now I'm lost. I thought there was a short cut through this industrial estate, but nothing looks familiar, and when I tried to backtrack I couldn't remember which buildings I had come past. Everywhere is empty and deserted, and the wind bangs against the side of the buildings, rattling the metal shutters, making me jump each time. I'm trying to switch my phone on when I hear it. It's so close I want to scream, but I know if I do, it will know where I am. I want to hide, but there's nowhere to go. So I run. I've dropped my phone but I don't care - I just need to run. I'm running so hard that my legs are burning, but suddenly the air around me feels too thick, too heavy, and I can't move fast enough.

But it can.

I can hear it behind me but I'm too afraid to look. It growls on every breath, and it sounds so angry at me. And all I want to do is run but it won't work and it feels like I'm falling, but I can't tell which way. It's so close now. I can feel it just behind me, and I know it's going to get my legs because I can't move them fast enough and it knows. And in a blind, furious panic I thrash my arms back behind me, trying to scare it away, trying to do anything to stop it getting me. I feel its mouth close over my hand and small, hot teeth puncture my arm. It's got me, oh god it's got me, and I can feel the blood rushing out of my arm, and I can feel it drinking, its jaws tightening on the bone. And as I feel the bone snap, I scream, so loud and so long that I think the whole world must be able to hear me.

***

"Justin! Justin, wake up!"

My heart was hammering so hard in my chest that it ached, and my skin was so clammy that it felt like I'd just had a shower. I tried to fight her off me, landing a blow to her head that made her reel back and cry out. She left me alone then, letting me come back slowly - the light from her bedside lamp, the sheets twisted around my feet. And as my breathing finally began to slow, I could see her properly. Karen, sitting at the bottom of our bed, holding her head and looking, what I shamefully realise as, afraid.

"Oh my god, Karen. I'm so sorry. I was dreaming again. Did I hurt you?"

I tried to sit up properly and move down the bed to her, but my legs had become too tightly wound up in the sheets. I reached down to untangle myself and started screaming. Karen jumped off the bed, backing away from me towards the door, hugging her arms around her body and looking more terrified than I ever wanted to see her.

"Justin! What is it? What's wrong?"

"My arm, what the hell happened to my arm?" I screamed, holding up my left arm to her, or rather what was left of it, as I stared in shock at the amputated stump.

"Justin stop it, you're scaring me!"

I can't understand why she won't come to me, why she won't help me.

"That thing, for fuck's sake, Karen that thing has eaten my arm!"

"It's not funny Justin, I mean it!" She sounded angry now, which was just confusing and making me angry as well. I couldn't think, I couldn't begin to understand what had happened and in the end all I could do was hold out my left arm to her, staring wide eyed, waiting for her to react.

"Yes, I know!" she shouted. "Fucking hell, Justin, we've been together four years and you think I haven't noticed before?"

I felt the room spin, the bed seemed to lurch underneath me, and I grabbed hold of the mattress with my other hand.

"What?"

Karen took a step towards the bed, her body relaxing slowly.

"I know it bothers you sometimes baby, but honestly, I'm fine with it. It's never affected how much I love you."

"But..." I started, feeling my skin go cold.

"Oh baby, did you have a bad dream? Come here." Karen climbed back onto the bed and cradled me in her arms, stroking and kissing my forehead. "Your mum told me once that you used to have bad dreams when you were little. But it's nothing to be ashamed of. It's just the way you were born."

"Just the way I was born," I mimicked back, my vision going blank.

"Shhh," whispered Karen, "it's OK. I told you on the day I met you – it doesn't matter to me."

***

When I woke up in the morning Karen was already downstairs getting ready. I felt groggy and drained, and for the briefest second I couldn't remember why, but then it came back, in sickening details. My heart started beating faster and faster and I was terrified to look, but in the end I forced my left arm up into view. It was gone. Just above the elbow, nothing but a smooth stump. I reached out to touch it with my other hand, but couldn't. Eventually I squeezed my left shoulder, and then down ever so slightly to the top of my arm. I could feel it, it was real. I kicked the sheets off my body and practically threw myself out of the bed. The floor was cold; we had bare floorboards and the heating wasn't on yet. I stamped on the floor, hard. My foot hurt. I stamped again, and then again. And then I slapped myself. My cheek stung and my ear was ringing.

"But this isn't…"

"Is that you baby? Breakfast is nearly ready."

"OK," I called back, too weakly for her to have heard.

I lifted my dressing gown off the back of the door. The left sleeve had been rolled up half way. I opened my wardrobe and pulled out three or four shirts, throwing them on to the bed. All of the left sleeves had been rolled up.

"Justin? Come on, it's getting cold!"

"Yeah, I'm coming," I said, feeling like I was losing my mind.

***

Once Karen had left for work, I quickly dressed and left the house. The doctor's surgery was about forty minutes' walk away – I made it in fifteen. Breathless and panting, I refused to leave until the receptionist agreed to squeeze me in with the doctor.

"Good morning, Mr. Glenn How can I help you this morning?"

Dr. Choudhary had been my GP since I was about fifteen, when Dad had relocated for work. He was a good man, smiling and patient no matter what the circumstances. As I walked into the examination room, I held up my left arm, waiting for the shock to hit him.

"Have you been experiencing some discomfort?"

"What?" I spat, "No, look! My arm is gone!"

"I'm well aware of that, Mr. Glenn Now how can I help?"

I fell into a chair, unable to control the scared, frustrated sobbing that now shook my body. Dr. Choudhary came around his desk and sat in the chair next to me, placing a hand on my shoulder and trying to calm me down. When I could finally speak again, I told him everything – the dreams, the thing chasing me, and waking up this morning missing my arm. He remained quiet the whole time, and when I had finished, he gave my shoulder a reassuring squeeze, then walked back around to his own chair.

"Mr. Glenn, I've known you for over fifteen years. I know this is scary for you at the moment, but I'm telling you the truth –

you were born missing your arm. I have your medical records on file; we can make an appointment to go through them if you wish, but I hope you trust that I wouldn't lie to you."

"But…" I didn't know what to say, I thought I knew the truth, but seeing how calm he was, how Karen had reacted – I had started to doubt myself.

"I don't want you to worry, Mr. Glenn. I'm sure that this sort of thing is more common than you'd think. I can give you something to help you sleep, but to be honest I don't think that will help in the long term. What I would like to do is refer you to a specialist, someone you can talk to about all of this. What do you think?"

"Yes, OK," I said, unable to look away

from the space where my left hand should have been.

***

The appointment card came through a week later. I was booked in for an assessment in six weeks time. Karen hadn't brought the subject up again, but I could feel it, silent and festering, driving a wedge between us. Maybe she hadn't noticed. I loved her, I really did, but I couldn't help myself. I didn't trust her anymore.

***

The field has been recently ploughed, the dark, rich soil sitting in regimented peaks and troughs that stretch out towards the horizon. There's nothing else, no trees or shrubs or houses for miles. I've been walking for hours, and I don't know how much farther I've got to go. It was light when I started, but the sun is going down now, and it's getting darker, and all I can think is I don't want to be out here in the dark. I thought I had some food with me, but I can't find it now and I'm hungry. It's fully dark now, there's no stars, no moon. It's like being inside, apart from the field. The dirt is loose and my feet keep slipping, making me tired. And the channels seem to be getting deeper; it's getting harder to climb up each side, and I can't see across the field anymore. I decide it's better to walk along one of the channels instead, I have to reach somewhere eventually.

And then, up ahead, I hear it. Soil and stones sliding down the steep sides, settling at the bottom somewhere just in front of me. And I know.

It's up there, watching me.

I freeze, ashamed of my fear, desperate to run, but I don't know which way to go. And then I hear it; it's sliding down the side, into the channel. I can't see it, it's too dark, but it's there, staring at me. I look from side to side; it's too steep, the soil too loose for me to climb. If I try that I'll get stuck. I turn and run as fast as I can. My feet pound into the soil, loose dirt and grit flying up all around me, sliding down the sides, burying my feet. It's not making any noise, but I know it's coming after me. It's toying with me, letting me stay ahead, letting me think I can get away.

The soil is falling down into the channel quicker now; it's up to my shins, and I can't pull my feet out quick enough. I try to scramble up one of the sides, but the dirt is too loose, it just comes down on top of me.

The impact knocks the air out of my lungs, and I fall onto my face, smelling the dirt, feeling the damp soil against my cheek. I can feel the full weight of it on my back, like a huge boulder, but squirming, thick hard bones digging into me, claws piercing the skin on my back. It's sizing me up, and I think if I just lay here as still as possible it will go away. I feel the weight shift and suddenly it's gone, my back and ribs aching from the pressure, and I'm just about to push myself upright when I feel it brush against my legs. And just as I think 'please don't ...' teeth rip into my thigh. My trousers feel wet and warm, like I've wet myself, but I know it's worse than that. It yanks backwards, my trousers shred and the back of my thigh tears away with it. I can feel it, feel the flesh leaving the bone, but it doesn't hurt. I hear it chew, once, twice, then feel its wet mouth close over my leg again, jaw tightening, bone snapping, and I can feel the wind blowing cold against the ragged wound. It licks the stump and my skin crawls. I feel clammy and sick.

And then I feel its teeth close around my other leg.

***

My eyes opened. The room was light so I knew it was morning. I could remember everything, feel everything. I felt so small, so helpless that I wanted to cry, or throw up. I felt so cold, and I couldn't stop shaking. I turned my head to look for Karen, but I was on the wrong side of the bed. I was on her side, not mine. But that didn't matter anymore, because I'd seen it. I'd seen it, and I knew. It had happened again. I felt sick and cold and I was shaking uncontrollably. But I couldn't tear my eyes away from it.

The wheelchair beside the bed.

My wheelchair.

***

I've been going through the motions with Karen for a few weeks now. She keeps bringing home brochures for new, electric chairs, and I nod my way through the conversations.

I found some old photographs last week, from holidays when I was a kid. Mum and Dad look the same, just as I'd always remembered them – Mum's bleached blonde hair and Dad's football shirts that he wore everywhere. My brother, Gavin, gap toothed smile as wide as his face. And then me.

Me on the beach.

Me by the swimming pool.

Me smiling with an ice cream.

Me in my wheelchair.

Me with one arm and both legs missing.

There were some baby photos as well, but I got drunk a few nights ago and tore them up. I hid the pieces at the bottom of the bin, so that Karen wouldn't find them.

I tried talking to the therapist, but she wasn't really listening to me. She kept saying I had unresolved anger regarding my situation and that it would help if I joined a local disability support group – speak to people in my position, see that life can still be rich and rewarding. She gave me a hand full of leaflets - coffee mornings, sports clubs and day centres. I binned the lot after our first session and didn't go back.

And then last night the dreams started again.

There's a clearing in the woods, but the trees have grown too close together, and I can't find a way through. I push and fight against the branches, but always give up, scratched and exhausted.

I know it's out there, in the woods somewhere, trying to find me. It's only a matter of time. It always finds me.

I've stopped telling Karen about the dreams. She always had the same look on her face, full of pity and soft, gentle understanding. But she doesn't believe me. I'm not even sure if I believe myself anymore. We've started arguing more and more, and yesterday I overheard her crying on the phone to her mum. Maybe there is something wrong with me, maybe it is delusions, or repressed anger. Maybe that thing in the woods is nothing but a sickness, deep in my mind, trying to confuse me.

I try to tell myself that every morning. Every time I wake up, my chest tight with panic, barely able to breathe, I tell myself over and over, it's only a dream. It's only a dream.

***

I can't see the trees anymore, everything has slipped away into blackness. It's cold, and the ground underneath my feet is slick with water. I want to stretch my arms out, to feel for the trees, for anything that might give me some kind of shelter, but I'm terrified. I strain my eyes, willing myself to see, but there's nothing. Just darkness, like I've fallen off the end of the world into nothing. I can hear wind in the tops of the trees, old branches creaking, threatening to snap.

I know it's out there. It's been out there for a while now, maybe forever. It doesn't make a sound, but I know it's coming. It doesn't need to make a noise anymore, that was all just to scare me. And it knows that I'm already as scared as I've ever been in my life. I can't move. I can't run or scream or fight anymore. The only thing I can do now is be afraid, and wait.

I can feel it in front of me, the heat

pulsing off its body. Hot, rancid breath surrounding me, making me gag. I try to scream, but nothing comes out, my face stretching out, pain biting into my cheeks at the strain of it. My heart feels like it has stopped, a lead weight in my chest, and I can feel the pressure of its breath all around me, turning the air bad, pushing against me, wrapping around every inch of me.

And in the blind, hot, fetid darkness I am repeating to myself;

Please wake up.

Please wake up.

Please…

***

Karen woke up, faint sunlight glowing around the edges of the curtains. Her head felt fuzzy, half-forgotten fragments of last night's dream fading already. She'd had a boyfriend, someone called James, or Justin? Something had been wrong… but it was gone, wiped clear with each blink as she came back around to consciousness. Looking at her bedside clock, Karen realised she was late, and she swore under her breath. She showered quickly and dressed for work; she would be lucky to make the bus on time.

She was ready to leave and paused for a moment in the kitchen, contemplating the bowl of fruit and various snack foods available, but on reflection she left it all untouched.

She wasn't feeling very hungry this morning.

First published in *Bramble and Other Stories*, Dale Parnell, 2019

RITUAL

By Kimberly Rei

The time was drawing nigh. Every nerve sang with the call of battle. He must prepare, and that meant pain. Blood.

He ran through the forest, trampling small trees and brush. Ritual required solitude.

Finally, there it was. The right tree, at the right height, with good, strong branches. He pulled in a deep breath, bracing himself for the trial to come.

The first scrape against wood shredded flesh from bone. Agony spread in a white-hot web. He leaned in, dragging again, and again. Skin hung in ragged tatters. Blood ran freely.

The sun was beginning to descend and still he stood, still he persevered. His enemies were near. He could smell them. They, too, were preparing, and he could not be caught unaware.

Only when the last slip of flesh stripped from bone, only when the final slither of blood fell to the forest floor, only then did he halt his ministrations and turn, lifting his head to scent the wind.

With a ruff of air and a hoof slapping the ground, the massive moose turned and went in search of his foe, his magnificent antlers clean and ready for war.

It was rutting season.

THE BUTCHER OF BLENGARTH

By David Bowmore

How do these tales of woe and misery usually start? With a creaking door, or the whistling wind, or even a blinking eye. Sometimes, they begin on a dark and wintery night.

***

On a dark winter's night with the threat of snow in the air, a figure carrying a backpack walks along a road wet with slushy, dirty snow. Wind whistles through the woods banked high above the traveller on either side of the road.

In this part of the world, street lighting does not connect one town with the next. Thick clouds obscure all illumination from the moon and stars. Fortunately, a torch held in one gloved hand provides limited light, making the journey slightly more bearable. The figure's shadow begins to grow and stretch ahead, as from behind an oncoming vehicle gains ground.

Turning, the figure extends an arm with the thumb raised. She blinks several times as the headlamps of the small, blue car pass by, leaving her once again in comparative darkness.

She isn't surprised. Who in their right mind would stop for a stranger on a night like tonight?

To her surprise, the car slows and eventually stops, evidently waiting for her to quicken her pace.

The window rolls smoothly down, and a warm feminine voice from within says, "Get in, then."

She stands back and opens the door with a loud creak that sends nesting birds scattering from their night's rest.

"Thanks," she says, sitting awkwardly with the backpack wedged between her legs.

"I'm going as far as Blengarth."

"That'll do. Thanks."

"Where're you headed?" the driver asks, changing gear.

"Anywhere, as far away as possible."

"There's a blizzard coming."

Snow begins to fall, proving her correct. She flicks a stick on her driving column to activate the wipers.

"Shit, really. I thought the worst was over."

She thinks she's upset the driver with her coarse language. The *swish-screee* of the rubber wipers highlights the silence settling inside the car.

"Don't you worry about picking up hitchhikers?" she asks.

"What do you mean?"

"You know, I might be a serial killer." She smiles to emphasise the joke.

"I see what you mean, but how do you know I'm not?"

The driver smiles at the look of surprise on the hitchhiker's face, then winks to let her know she's pulling her leg.

"Only joking. Name's Mira."

"Hi. Janet," says the hitchhiker offering her hand. They shake awkwardly.

The flakes of snow increase in size and begin to lay thick on the bonnet of the car. The windscreen wipers flick the wet splotches faster. Mira turns the heating up.

"I hate this stretch of road," she says.

"The council never seems to spread grit here."

The back end slides as they round a tight curve, causing Janet to close her knees tight on the backpack.

"Don't worry. You're safe—trust me. Are you running from someone?

"You can tell?"

"Who sets out on a night like this without planning?"

Janet fiddles with the toggles at the top of her bag. Taking a deep breath, she says, "Yes, I'm running. The situation with my partner is over. He won't accept it. I tried leaving once before, and he broke a mug of tea over my head, he did. I needed stitches."

"Shit!" Mira throws a concerned

glance out of the corner of her eye.

"Sorry, I shouldn't off-load on you."

"Doesn't matter. Sometimes a stranger is the best person to talk to. If you ask me, you're doing the right thing. Men—they're all bastards."

Silence settles between them again. Mira has to slow the car as the snowfall becomes increasingly thicker, making it difficult to see the front of the bonnet.

"So, he doesn't know you've gone yet?"

"No, I'll get word to him in a day or two."

"I'm sorry." She hunches over the steering wheel as if being closer to the windscreen will help her to see further.

"When you're not picking up

runaways, what do you do?"

"Me? I'm a butcher."

"Oh—you don't see many women butchers."

"I know it's not a normal trade for us to seek out, but believe me, I do the job as well as any man."

"It will be a long time before men believe that."

Mira takes her eyes off the road for a second to share a sympathetic smile, then says, "Jesus, this snow. Can you believe it?"

"How far from town now?"

"Less than a mile. What will you do once I drop you off?"

"Not sure. Find a B&B for the night, take the first bus to anywhere in the morning."

"You won't find anywhere open in Blengarth at this time of night, and all the pubs will be closed, too. Tell you what— you can sleep on my sofa. Us girls must stick together."

"I couldn't."

"Don't be silly. What else you going to do? You can get a bus in the morning."

"That's very kind of you, but won't your husband mind?"

"Divorced."

"Oh, sorry."

"Don't be. I caught him with his dick in the bacon slicer."

"Eaurgh!"

"So I sacked her too." Mira lets out a chortle, slapping the palm of her hand against the wheel.

"Oh, I see…"

"No, I'm sorry. It's a butcher's joke. Still want my sofa?"

"Yes, please."

***

In the warmth of her apartment, over the butcher's shop, Mira pours them each a glass of red wine and crouches to light the gas fire with a match. *Click, click, click, whoomp.* Blue flames dance over the ceramic heating tiles covered in mesh. She tosses the dead wood into a saucer on the hearth.

Janet sits on the sofa that will be her bed for the night. Her bag rests in the corner of the small room. Mira has already found a blanket for her to sleep under.

Mira sits opposite, and Janet sees her properly for the first time. Large round eyes look back at her. Mira tucks a strand of dark hair behind her ear. Both corners of her lips rise in a suggestive smile, before looking away. She fiddles with a heavy piece of stone jewellery around her neck. Even wearing a thick sweater, the shapely outline of her body is hard to ignore.

What is she telling Janet? Is she imagining the signs? Even so, this is too close to home; she needs to be far away from John. If she gives into base instincts, she might stay another night, and then another. It wouldn't be difficult for John to find her.

"It's been a long day, Mira. Would it be okay if I turn in?"

"Sure. I'm just across the passage if you want anything," she says, running the tip of her tongue over her lips.

"I'm sorry?"

"Relax, I'm teasing you…just a little. It's been a while since anyone was in my apartment, let alone my bed; I'm not sure I'd know what to do."

Mira finishes her drink, leaving a lipstick imprint on the rim, and stands to leave. She smiles with her whole body.

"Sleep well."

She leans down and leaves a lingering kiss on Janet's cheek.

Now Janet knows all she has to do is tap on Mira's bedroom door, and she won't be turned away.

Janet also knows her hostess is a strange one. Her jokes are a bit too sick or off-kilter. Laughing about her ex-husband having an affair. Who does that?

And surely she's a little too keen. They're complete strangers. Is she really that easy?

But those eyes.

Janet drains her glass, savouring the warm fuzzy glow filling her. Still clothed, she stretches out on the sofa. The blanket doesn't cover her feet.

Now, she hears the shower running.

It's only one night, Jan. You'll be gone in the morning. Grab the nettle and explore that side of your nature you've denied for so long.

Janet's need forms a knot at the pit of her stomach. She'll go to her. After all, they're both consenting adults and can deal with things in the appropriate way.

"Would it be wrong to want to share your bed for the night? After all, what harm is there in two lonely people bringing a little happiness to each other, even if it is only for one night?"

These words are fine inside your head, Jan. But when you say them out loud, you'll sound like a silly twat from a bad romance novel.

The shower comes to a trickling stop. *Now or never, Jan.*

She steps into the passageway as Mira, loosely wrapped in a towelling robe, opens the bathroom door.

"Sorry," Janet says, all bravery gone in an instant.

"Don't be. I usually read for an hour or so. Don't worry about disturbing me. Let me know if I can do anything for you."

Mira's dark eyes are peering deep into her soul, reading her heart, and understanding her needs.

All Janet has to do is make the move. She takes a step closer; she has an ache which needs rubbing.

"Well, I was wondering…ah…if… well…"

Janet can smell honey rising from Mira's warm body.

"Yes, Janet? What is it? What do you want?"

The doorbell rings, long and shrill,

making them both jump a little.

"Ignore it," Mira says, stepping closer.

"Ask me." Janet reaches a hand forward. Their fingers touch. Janet's eyes close. Her lips tremble.

The doorbell rings again, followed by loud, insistent banging.

"I'll get rid of whoever it is," Mira says.

***

The first thing Janet is aware of when she wakes is the pain at the front of her head. Her right eye, throbbing in time with her forehead, refuses to open. She tries to touch it, only to realise her wrists are tied to the arms of a wooden chair. She can feel ropes biting into her torso and legs, making it impossible to move. Nonetheless, she rocks the chair from side to side.

"Help!"

It occurs to her that the darkness is not due to her inability to open one eye, and surely she shouldn't be cold enough for her teeth to chatter. She pauses in her rocking to assess the situation.

She can feel the rough wooden slates of the chair pinching her naked behind.

"Oh, God."

The memory surfaces. She and Mira were seconds from embracing. Mira had gone to answer the door then Janet heard her call out. The door had slammed shut and by the time she got to the top of the stairs, John was already halfway up as Mira slumped by the front door with blood pumping from her head. Janet was too stunned to say anything as his baton struck and darkness descended.

The rope has cut into her wrists, grating on her nerve endings with every convulsive shiver.

"John." Her voice cracks.

Clunk—the door opens. She blinks her good eye as the light of the walk-in refrigerator winks into life. Warm air rushes in, causing the motors of the cold box to engage with a whining, whistling drone.

John stands before her, tapping his extendable baton in the palm of his left hand. He has taken off his bulkier outerwear - jacket, body armour and helmet.

One of his cheeks is splashed with blood.

"Please stop this, John."

"Did you really think you could ever leave me, Janet?"

"I'm sorry. I'll come home. It won't happen again."

"I don't believe you. You're sorry now because you're scared, but what about later when you're feeling strong? If you come home, you'll soon return to your old habits, because ultimately you're weak and without moral fortitude."

"I won't. I promise."

"You will. Thinking impure thoughts, imagining unnatural acts, and looking at girls like this one tonight."

"Nothing happened. She gave me a lift. That's all."

"Liar!" The crack of the steel baton on the inside of the door reverberates around the box, sending a jolt of fear right through her. "What were you doing in her flat?"

"She was only letting me sleep on her sofa. Because the weather is so bad. That's all."

"You are a liar." John steps inside and turns her face with the cold steel of the baton under her chin. "Her lipstick betrays you."

"What? No, no, no it wasn't like that—Arghhhh!"

"I think you may have broken your arm on my trusty truncheon, dearest. Keep lying to me and I'll be forced to find other ways to hurt you."

Janet nods her head, tries to still her rattling teeth. Tears and snot mingle with sticky blood.

"You realise you're in the refrigerator at the back of a butcher's shop. No one can hear you scream."

"Please, nothing happened."

"Of course," he continues, "being a butcher's, they have lots of very sharp knives here. What fun we can have? Don't move. I'll be back in a minute." He backs out of the box, leaving the door open.

She can hear John grunting as something weighty is dragged and moved. Then a loud heavy thud followed by a whimper and groan. Despite the cold, her forehead prickles with dots of perspiration.

John returns to the doorway, a cleaver in one hand and something small in the palm of the other.

"I found this cleaver. They have hammers and pliers too. And big machines for slicing and mincing. So, tell me what happened, before I feed her to you, piece by piece."

"Nothing happened. I promise. I just wanted a bed for the night."

"What happened?" John steps into the fridge, dropping the cleaver and grabbing Janet's face with his left hand.

"Tell me."

"Nothing—God's honest truth."

He forces Mira's severed fingertip into Janet's mouth, pushing her jaw closed around it.

"Swallow it! Swallow, you bitch."

He pinches her nostrils closed. Blood fills her mouth, the fingernail tickles her tonsils. She can't breathe and gags as she tries not to swallow.

She loses control of her bladder and warm liquid floods the chair, dripping onto the floor. John steps away, his lips curled in a cruel smirk as Janet coughs and spits the digit onto her bare thighs.

"You need help, John. I'll help you find it. I won't leave you. I promise."

"She was in her robe. What did you see?"

"Nothing." She was still spitting to try to clear her mouth of Mira's blood. "I saw nothing! We did nothing."

"Liar. You wanted to, didn't you?

Admit it," he says, once again withdrawing from the torture chamber.

"Please stop, John, please. Remember you're a policeman."

John returns, holding a knife with a long, pointed blade.

"Now, let's make sure you never see anything again, you cheating, lying deviant," he says.

Once again, he grabs her face with his left hand and begins to lower the point of the knife towards Janet's left eye. She closes the eyelid tight in a feeble attempt to protect her sight.

"Please. Don't. I'm begging you—" Her words becoming a soul searing scream as the sharp point easily cuts through the thin skin of her eyelid, making contact with the orb underneath. He drags the tip across to the outer edge and finally releases her face from his tight grip. Blood pumps down her cheek. Her breaths are short, quick, and filled with sobs.

The pain is exceptional. She knows agony like this cannot be sustained for long, and that she will die from the pain alone. She doesn't see or feel anything as John wipes his thumb over her exposed and bloody eyeball. But she does endure the shooting, tearing pain as he tugs at her eyelid, which dangles by a few millimetres of flesh.

"I've only scratched the surface, darling," he says in soothing tones, while stroking her bloody cheek. "Now, don't struggle. You'll only make things worse, although I really don't see how things could get much worse for you. I am, after all, about to hack your eyeball to shreds."

"P…please…don't…"

She can't see anything clearly, with one eye swollen shut and the other damaged beyond usefulness. But she does hear a sound like an egg cracking, followed by the full weight of John slumping forward against her. The knife he holds slices most of her ear off then clatters to the floor. She feels her shoulder become slick with blood.

A vague shadowy bloody figure stands before Janet. A large crusted bruise has formed in the middle of her forehead. One hand is wrapped in a bloody tea-towel while the other holds a heavy mallet, the ridged metal surface matted with blood and hair.

"Pig," Mira screams as she brings the metal mallet down for a second time, caving in the front of John's head. One more blow brings his convulsions to a halt.

"Oh my God. Is that you, Mira? Please tell me it's you? Talk to me. I'm so sorry. Are you okay?"

Mira's eyes shift from the uniformed body on to the floor to the bonds holding Janet to the chair.

"It's me." Her voice has lost all its previous warmth.

"Untie me. Then call the police. We need help."

"No," Mira replies.

"No?"

"I've got you just where I wanted you all along. Human flesh tastes very much like pork."

Before Janet can fully comprehend her meaning, Mira steps back out of the fridge, silencing the rising screams by shutting the heavy door.

First published in *Full Metal Horror 2*, Zombie Pirate Publishing, 2019

DEAD FACES

By R.J. Meldrum

The woman was young and very pretty. Her face was serene, her eyes closed. She sat in the driver's seat of a car that lay on its side in a ditch. A trickle of blood from her ear was the only indication she was dead. Her head had shattered the windshield.

Jim hated car accidents, but it was his job to photograph these incidents on behalf of the police.

He focused his camera onto the corpse. As he stared through the viewfinder, the woman's eyes flicked open and her mouth moved. A voice spoke in his head.

It was a drunk driver. He drove me off the road.

Jim closed his eyes, feeling nauseous. It was happening again. He waited a few seconds, then reopened his eyes. The woman was a corpse once more. He carried on, photographing the scene.

It'd started about two months before. The first time had terrified him. A young man, sprawled dead on the road after a street robbery. There was a small round hole in his chest, ringed with dried blood. His back was a gaping chasm of exposed muscle, bone and organs. His killer had used a large-caliber weapon. As Jim had bent to take the photograph, the corpse opened his eyes and his mouth formed words.

I was shot for my cell phone.

There had been a thunderbolt of pain in Jim's head. He had staggered. A nearby police officer had to steady him before he fell. Afterwards he reasoned it'd been a simple hallucination, brought on by stress.

As the weeks passed and the dead continued to speak to him, he began to realise it was real. Looking down the viewfinder of his camera allowed him an insight into these peoples' deaths. He thought back to the words he'd heard over the last few weeks.

A woman whose throat had been cut open with a kitchen knife.

My husband did this. He cut me open and watched me bleed.

A teenager, bloated and pale, recovered from a river after five days in the water.

I drowned myself. I wanted to die.

A man impaled on a metal fence post.

I fell off my motorbike. I felt the metal pierce my heart.

The stories accumulated in his mind, his memory unable to delete them, but there was still one type missing from his unique collection. He knew it was going to be unbearable when he was required to photograph that particular scene.

It was a dark, wet night when the police phoned, requesting his attendance at a house on the south side. He asked the particulars, even though he wasn't supposed to. The officer spoke the words he dreaded to hear. Infanticide.

He replaced the receiver. It had finally happened; the one corpse he'd dreaded since this all started. He stood, opened the drawer of his desk and removed the coiled rope. He'd prepared for this, knowing he couldn't bear to see a tiny mouth speak of atrocities and horror. He hung the rope from the hook he'd drilled into the ceiling, placed the noose around his neck and stood on his chair. With a sense of relief, he kicked it away.

First published in *The Sirens Call eZine*, Sirens Call Publications, 2017

PIG MAN

By Stephen Herczeg

Halloween. Best night of the year. Especially on the strip. The red of the traffic lights makes the scattered puddles look like pools of blood. Like the slick smears I leave behind when I finish with my victims.

Tonight there are more choices than ever. Nubile, young things parade along the street. Long legs, big breasts, tight asses. Dressed as sexy Vampires, sexy Zombies, sexy Nurses. They're all sexy. I want 'em all.

I feel something stirring. Gotta keep myself calm. Don't let the little head get in the way of the big head.

It happened the first time. She was a real beauty. Legs that went on forever. Blonde hair that fell all the way down her back. Huge perky breasts. An ass you could crack walnuts with.

I couldn't control myself. I grabbed her off the street when she stopped to fix her shoe. She was feisty, which made her more irresistible. She bit the hand clamped over her mouth. She kicked me. Scratched me. I loved every second of it.

I dragged her down the alley. The gaudy neons painted us in strange hues. Sickly yellow one moment. Blood red the next. Decaying green another. The lights think it's Halloween every night.

She kept attacking. Punched me. Struggled in my arms. I managed to pull one of my knives out and held it in front of her face. She stopped. Her eyes transfixed by the reflected lights off the blade. Then started again. I was forced back and tripped with her on top of me. She stayed still. When I pushed her off, the knife was ripped out of my hand. I sat up and saw the handle poking out of her chest.

Damn. Over too soon.

From that day on I kept myself in check. The pleasure comes from taking my time. Not rushing, and not too often—that will bring the cops. The urge came every few months at first, of late it's been more frequent, but I keep a lid on it. Pick my moments. Pick my victims. Pick my locations. And really enjoy it when it happens.

Halloween is the best. I can camp out on the strip in full display. No-one looks twice at my bloodied butcher's apron, my set of knives in their scabbard, the cleaver that hangs from my belt and most of all, my Pig mask. The beauties look and laugh as if I'm just another reveller. I smile back and leer at them. Watching. Scrutinising.

Choosing.

And then I see tonight's victim. A gorgeous Asian beauty dressed as a scarlet ninja. I smile at her. Our eyes meet and she smiles back. She stops and falls behind her group of friends. She sizes me up for a moment then walks over.

"Hello, Mr Pig Butcher man," she says in a thick accent. She peers down the alley I stand before. "What you hiding down here?"

She steps into the shadows and walks deep into the bowels of the laneway. She is consumed by the darkness. I can't quite believe my luck. I look around for any witnesses. The party goers continue on with their self-destruction. I turn and fall in behind her.

As we reach the end of the passageway, I draw a long filleting knife and hold it out before me. A quick cut to the leg should disable my little ninja, then the real fun can begin.

She stops.

"Are you the same Mr Pig Butcher man been killing here for a few years?"

My mouth drops open.

"How? How?"

"I been watching for a while. You kill my sister three years ago."

Shocked into self-preservation, I step forward, ready to drive the knife home.

She turns. The two blades she holds look very sharp. As they plunge into my chest, they feel very sharp indeed. I collapse backwards. She steps into view.

The last thing I see is her smiling face as she stares down. The darkness collects me.

First published in *Tricksters Treats #1*, Things in the Well Press, 2017

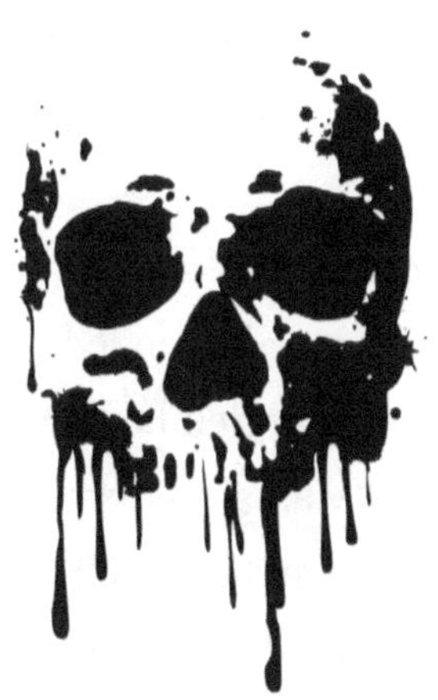

SINISTER CHANGELING

By Zoey Xolton

Vera was born mute they said. It wasn't true, of course. She was brighter, and more gifted than the lot of her pathetic, backwater family. Where they were robust, blue-eyed and blonde, she was pale, with dark, slanted eyes, hair, and an even darker mind.

She *chose* her silence.

As her mama descended the creaking staircase, Vera wiggled her fingers, malice on her mind. Mama gasped, and tripped, tumbling head over heels. When she finally lay twisted, bloody, and broken on the landing…Vera burst out laughing.

Her 'family' stared in horror.

The Unseelie Court would be glad of her return.

First published in *Hawthorn & Ash*, Iron Faerie Publishing, 2019

LOCKDOWN HORROR #1

ABOUT THE PUBLISHER

BLACK HARE PRESS is a small, independent publisher based in Melbourne, Australia.

Founded in 2018, our aim has always been to champion emerging authors from all around the globe and offer opportunities for them to participate in speculative fiction and horror short story anthologies.

Connect

Website: *www.blackharepress.com*

Twitter: *@BlackHarePress*